# Saving the Bellydancer

## Green Brotherhood: Seal Team XII
### Book 3

### Debra Parmley

# Dedication

*For "Sabeya" aka Francesca Sabeya Anastasi, founder of
International Shimmy Mob,
and for all my Shimmy Mob bellydance sisters.*

*It has been an honor, to found Shimmy Mob Memphis, in the
inaugural Shimmy Mob held on May 1st, 2011. Each year, I
get goosebumps, seeing my sisters all over the world dance.
Each of you are a shining light and together we light up this
globe. I thank you with all of my heart.*

*It is to each of you, my dance sisters, shining your lights,
along with Sabeya, that I dedicate this book,
Saving the Bellydancer.*

*May your light always shine*

# Chapter One

2011

Little Creek, Virginia

Navy SEAL Antonius (Tony) "Cutter" Cuttino slid his six-foot frame behind the wheel of his red Corvette. Starting the car up and then shifting gears, he pulled the car out of the garage, and down the driveway, before backing into the street.

As he headed to Chicks Oyster Bar, he thought about his buddy's upcoming wedding.

*Cutter getting married will change everything.*

Change, however, was a part of life.

Chicks Oyster Bar, located at the Marina, was a big SEAL hangout. This was where the guys would throw the bachelor party. Many SEALs married bartenders or waitresses they'd met there, and women looking to meet a SEAL knew it was a possibility that one of the fit, handsome guys who frequented the bar was a SEAL.

Cutter had met his share of women at the bar, but none of those get togethers had lasted more than a month. He hadn't been looking for anything long term. He'd entered the Navy, wanting to see the world first, without having to worry about a family, or a permanent girlfriend.

His grandmother was still living, and other than a large group of cousins, she was the only family he had in the states to come back to. His job as a SEAL suited his adventurous soul.

Still fit, and mentally sharp, his grandmother had her circle of friends and stayed busy, though she was always happy to hear from Tony, or be surprised by his visits.

Thinking of her, he reminded himself to call her tomorrow, before the day was over.

Reed Tindall "Railroad" aka "R.T." would soon be getting married to Christie Anderson, a cute little floral designer who worked at Floral Blessings. R.T. had lucked out meeting Christie. With her blonde hair and curves, she looked like a gorgeous pin-up girl, and wearing 1940's style dresses and heels which was her big hobby.

If Cutter had been as lucky as R.T., and met a woman like Christie, he might have considered a permanent relationship too. He wouldn't want her to get away.

Glad he hadn't met the woman of his dreams yet; he was happy for his friend.

After Becky, the girl who'd sent him a chickenshit Dear John letter, Cutter made sure none of the girls he dated lasted longer than a month. He had fun, he treated women right, but he wasn't about to get tied down. He made it clear that their fun was for a short time only. Anything else was a deal breaker. He wasn't about to get his heart broken again by another damn letter.

It was easier for a SEAL not to have a girl to worry

about back home. There were women to be found in every port in the world. It wasn't as if he lacked female companionship. Being a SEAL, and a tall dark and handsome Italian American, he drew women like a magnet.

R.T. had been a carefree single man too, until meeting Christie. Then no other woman caught his eye. That was a sign, if anything were, that they were meant to be. But the couple had an unusual first meeting story.

They'd met at the movie premiere of the Cole Kennick movie, Stand and Deliver, when they'd sat next to each other. A live shooter had entered the building.

R.T. had taken out the shooter, and then had to apply tourniquets to two men, before they bled out.

He'd saved Christie's life, and then talked her through applying the second tourniquet, to save the second man's life. The way she'd handled herself, had him seeing a side to her that drew him in, beyond her blonde bombshell looks.

Afterward, he'd seen her safely home. From that night on, they'd dated constantly, and she became the only woman Railroad was interested in.

Christie kept saying it was the worst and the best day of her life. While it wasn't R.T.'s worst, he never talked to her about the worst day of his life, he agreed with Christie that it was the best day of his life too.

Cutter had been with R.T. on the worst day of his life, and had been one of the ones to save R.T. One of the team. They'd been on that mission together, and all come home together, which was nothing short of a miracle. It had knit them all tighter together than anything else would, or could have, and that bond of brotherhood was now unbreakable.

Each man would be celebrating this wedding with everything a SEAL had in him, because each knew how short and precious life could be. This meant it was going to be one hell of a party. For many reasons.

First was the theme. The bridal party would all be wearing 1940's style clothing.

Cutter looked forward to seeing the ladies dolled up, and to swing dancing which sounded like fun. He'd never done any swing dancing, but Christie had arranged for an evening lesson for the whole wedding party.

Cutter was a quick learner, like most SEALs.

He'd have yet another skill to add to the ever-growing list of things he knew how to do. Watching his grandmother in her thirst for learning, he knew it was a lifestyle, and a way of thinking, that would keep him young. She seemed younger than her age, and her high spirits had a youthful way to them.

Tonight, he was meeting the guys at the bar, and getting the scoop on what else was planned for the bachelor party they were all looking forward to. It would, of course, be at Chicks, and involve shots, stories, and maybe a challenge or two.

* * *

Partnered with one of Christie's 1940's group friends, Cutter looked forward to dancing. He watched as the first couple, who taught the dances, demonstrated the dance they'd be learning.

*Swing dancing was well named.*

He watched the couple swing around the floor, the man swinging the smaller woman, as if she weighed hardly a thing.

R.T. had a great big grin on his face, as he looked at his fiancé.

She wore a glow which was undeniable. Anyone viewing the scene, could have picked out the bride to be, as they both were clearly in love, and she wore that glow that well-loved women often take on.

R.T. couldn't keep his hands off her, something Cutter wasn't used to seeing. It made him grin. *They were like a couple of teenagers.*

Cutters dance partner was a dark-haired girl with blue eyes. He'd always been drawn to dancers, loved their legs, and the way they moved, so normally his dance partner would've held his attention and interest, but their chemistry was off, and her high-pitched laugh grated on his nerves more than a little.

But when the music started, he set that aside and concentrated on learning the dance steps and moves, so he could swing his partner around the room.

At the end of the hour, it hadn't been so bad. He'd kept her busy dancing, not chatting, and the hour was up. It had been fun.

Though he'd be paired with whoever Christie desired to pair him with from the wedding party, he wouldn't be escorting her as his date. He'd find a date.

*There was time.*

Too bad he couldn't be paired with Tanya, Christies best friend who was beautiful, and fun to talk to. But she already had a boyfriend, so that was a no go.

It wasn't as if he had trouble getting dates. He'd find someone.

* * *

Local belly dancer "Zarifah" entered the dance studio late. She'd missed troupe rehearsal, and was supposed to stay afterward, to practice her veil solo, where she could use the two walls of mirrors and the large space.

Her apartment was much too small to spin around in with a veil, without knocking things over, and she couldn't do that anymore. Not with the porcelain figurines Hassan had given her decorating the rooms.

The beautiful gifts were too expensive, and treasured by her, to risk them, so she no longer danced in her apartment, even without a veil. She missed dancing there.

Amina, the studio owner and troupe director, saw her coming through the door and said, "I wondered where you were," then she took a few steps toward her, a frown coming over her face as she took a closer look, and saw bruises covering the left side of Zarifah's face. "Honey, what happened to you? Are you all right?"

"He came back. Last night." She spoke quiet, though there was no one else in the studio to hear her. It was still hard, sharing what had happened, even with one of her closest friends.

"Oh no. Honey, who did that to you?" Their eyes met, and then Amina's eyes widened, as she realized who had done it. "Hassan."

"Yes." Zarifah nodded. "Luckily, my neighbor, Mrs. Dieter, called the police. Or I might not be here with you tonight. He was so very angry."

"Come in," Amina gently touched her elbow, to guide her in, and then pulled her hand back, as if afraid she might hurt her. "Was that okay? I don't want to touch you where it hurts."

"Yes. I'll be fine. I'm just a bit beat up at the moment." She gave a slight shrug.

Though this was a different kind of bruising, Zarifah had grown accustomed to bruises left by gymnastics, when she was young and still learning. Her sights set on the Olympics, she and her coaches had pushed her hard back then.

*Bruising happened. You got over it.*

She set her jaw, summoning that determination which she'd learned at a young age while training for the Olympics.

Amina pulled a chair around for her. "Sit. Rest. I'll make us some tea. Then I want you to tell me what happened."

"Okay." Zarifah sat, but didn't relax in the chair. She hadn't relaxed, since the night the man she'd thought she loved, who she thought had loved her, had turned into a monster. She wondered if she would ever relax again.

Amina loved tea, and any excuse to make it. Tonight was no exception. "Chamomile this evening, I think. It's a soothing tea. Sound good?"

Zarifah nodded, and then watched her friend, as she readied the small, portable tea maker, pouring water into it, before starting the water to boil. Once the tea was ready, Amina would want her to tell everything that had happened with Hassan.

*Hopefully the bruises will be gone before our next perfor-mance. If not, I'll have to bow out. Hassam will get his wish, if I'm not dancing. I don't want anyone taking photos, or video of me looking like this.*

She had to tell Amina, and she also needed to tell her that Hassan was dangerous, in case he ever showed up near any of the other dancers.

They were used to him, and wouldn't see him as dangerous, so everyone needed to be told. It wouldn't be right to keep it private, and keep them in the dark.

Security at the venues in their dance schedule wouldn't

have seen him before. She'd run through the list of places in her head, on the drive over, to remember if he'd ever come to watch her dance at any of them. He hadn't.

She wished she hadn't burned all her pictures of him last night, and blocked him on social media, when she'd been too upset to think she might need one photo of him. She'd been thinking she never wanted to see his face again.

They would have to find a picture of him somewhere, somehow. To give to security.

*Maybe Amina can help.*

It was important that all their dance sisters be safe.

* * *

Cutter was running late, for the first half of the bachelor party, at the Sweet Kitty Kat Club, and didn't want to miss the main event. They would watch the girls, and then move on to Chicks, for drinking games and hot chicks.

Being on the SEAL teams meant you could be called away on short notice, for a good long time, and called away often. That made it hard on girlfriends, fiancés and wives. RT had worried that Christie might not be able to deal with the lifestyle. But she was sure she wanted this. Time would tell, but they had a good chance of making it last.

Christie was a good woman. R.T. had made a wise choice in her. She was a real cutie, with her retro pinup outfits, and good girl next-door good looks.

The wedding party would be in Navy dress uniforms for the men, and the women would be in vintage dresses, like Marilyn Monroe would have worn. The kind that showed off all their curves. Cutter was all for that look, and looking forward to all the eye candy at the wedding.

He couldn't have been happier for the couple. RT was

happier than Cutter had ever seen him, and Cutter could envision the two of them as a happily married gray haired couple in their twilight years together. He wanted that too, when he grew old.

But that was far into the future. He was living in the now, the today. Because that was all anyone ever really had.

Tonight, Cutter was running late to the party, but with any luck, the headline dancer wouldn't have started yet. He enjoyed watching dancers, with their long legs that could wrap around a man, and their toned bodies, which moved in ways that made him think of moving with them in a more intimate way across the sheets.

*Dancers were hot. This first half of the party at the strip club should be good.*

He sped up, his mind on long legged females stripping.

While he was glad for R.T., and their other buddy, SEAL Tanner "Diesel" Taylor who had a wife and two kids now, he wasn't ready to find his own wife and settle down. He was too busy having fun in between deployments. Dating strippers was part of that fun.

* * *

The next morning, Tony's cell phone rang, the vibration mode making it dance on the nightstand.

He reached for the phone. His eighty-year-old grandmother was calling, so he answered. "Good morning, grandma," he said, as he glanced at the stripper sleeping next to him in his bed.

"So Tony, when are you going to come home and see your grandmamma?" his grandmother asked.

"Who's on the phone, baby?" Tawny asked. She ran her hand up his thigh. "Come here."

His grandmother kept on as if she hadn't heard the woman. "Nicki has three babies already, and you never even married."

He turned away from Tawny, stood up and walked away, holding up a finger to her to wait. "Yes, Grandma, I know. Nicki has a new baby every year. I'm happy for her. She deserves the best."

Nicki was a neighborhood girl he'd dated in high school.

Tawny got out of bed, and started pulling her clothes on.

He watched her naked body, as she covered it with clothes, while he listened to his grandma.

Tawny had a great body. Long, sexy legs. Big breasts that bounced. She'd also gotten drunk last night, after they got to his place, and had been wild, as strippers often were. One thing he liked about them.

He rolled his left shoulder, feeling the scratches she'd made across his back. Those long silver painted fingernails of hers were killer. He'd made her scream a few times. Noisy sex that could wake the neighbors.

He walked into the other room, to be further away from her, as he talked to his grandmother, so he could pay better attention to his grandmother as she continued to talk.

"When you gonna get married, Tony. I want to be holding my own great grandbabies, not somebody else's," his grandmother said. "You gonna get yourself killed, doing all that crazy stuff. I want you home soon. Marry. Have lots of babies."

He laughed. "Grandma, I'm not ready for marriage yet. The girl has to be the right girl, you know?"

"I know you're too picky," she said. "What one you have there with you this morning? Is she even Italian?"

Tawny was a hot blonde, with blue eyes, and was not

the kind of girl he would bring home to meet his grandmother.

*Definitely not Italian.*

"Not Italian. I need to take her home, grandma. I'll call you later on today."

"Okay, Tony," she said. "But don't forget about your old grand-mamma."

"I would never forget about you, grandma. And you are not old. I'm planning to visit you soon. We can talk later."

"Okay, you go and take that one home. Then find one you can marry. I'm not getting any younger, you know."

"I love you grandma," he said.

"I love you too, Tony boy."

"Talk to you soon, grandma. Bye bye."

"Okay, bye bye." She hung up the phone, and then he hung up.

She was only person he knew that he said, 'bye bye' to. After his parents had passed, his grandma was all the family he had.

An only child, it was up to him to carry on the family name, and give his grandmother some grand-babies to fuss over. She was right; he did need to visit her. But not with a potential wife. He could fly home for a weekend, and then fly back. He had plenty of leave, and as she'd said, she wasn't getting any younger.

When he got back to Tawny, she'd crossed her arms, and was giving him the stink eye expression. Why, he didn't know, as he'd thought the sex was good last night, for both of them.

"So your real name is Tony?" Tawny said. "Is there a reason you told me your name is Cutter, not Tony?"

"That is my name. They're both my names. Call me Cutter," he said.

"But your grandma calls you Tony," she said.

"That's right."

She took out a cigarette and lit it. Something she hadn't done last night. But he'd realized once they were naked in bed, that she was a smoker. Because smoke wasn't just on her clothes from working in the club. Once she removed all her clothes, and he began kissing her skin and her lips, he could taste that she was a smoker.

He would never marry a woman who smoked. It was a real turn off for him. He regretted inviting her back to his place last night.

Maybe his grandmother was right, he needed to start dating a different kind of woman.

"I'm ready to go," she said. "You gonna buy me breakfast?"

"Sure." He reached for his keys. "Where do you want to go?"

"There's a waffle place, around the corner from the club."

"Okay." He nodded. "Let's go." He'd feed Tawny, drop her off at her car, say goodbye, and then, make sure she drove away safely. But first, since he needed a date for the wedding, and he was out of time, he'd ask her if she'd like to go.

She seemed to have a thing for SEALs, and had mentioned she'd dated a SEAL before. Then she'd peeled off her top, revealing those marvelous breasts, and walked toward him. Watching them bounce, he'd forgotten about her comment.

Now he wondered who the guy was.

* * *

"Here you go." Amina handed Zarifah a cup of hot tea. Sitting back in her chair, she put her full attention on Zarifah. "Now, tell me everything. From the beginning. I only knew that you had called off your engagement to Hassan."

"From the beginning." Zarifah took a deep breath. "Okay." She nodded. "The reason I called off our engagement," she frowned, paused, and then decided to start over.

Amina patiently waited for her to get on with the story.

"From the moment Hassan put the ring on my finger, everything changed," Zarifah said. "He changed. It was as if he was a different person."

"Oh no," Amina said.

"He did *not* want me dancing." Zarifah frowned.

"He didn't? I thought Hassan loved your dancing," Amina said. "He was always enthusiastic, usually clapping the loudest, and he came to all our shows, and was encouraging afterward." Amina's face showed her surprise.

Apparently, Hassan had fooled her too.

"Oh, he loves it all right. But only for him." Zarifah shook her head. "He said I would only dance in private, for him, from now on. And, from now on, meant, right this minute. Not after we got married, not after the shows I've already committed to."

"If you need to pull from a show, I will understand," Amina said. "It's okay. Just keep coming to the studio to dance with us. We would miss you terribly if you left."

"No, that's not what I need," Zarifah shook her head and frowned. "Hassan is unreasonable. *He* is the problem. He insisted I would not wear a belly dance costume, outside of his house, or ever dance in public again, after we were engaged."

"Ah. His Middle Eastern upbringing is coming out." Amina nodded. "That's how he was raised. Wives don't dance, except in private at home, or with other women. Not even at weddings. The only dancers there are the hired belly dancers. He doesn't understand it's different here, in the United States. These are cultural differences."

"Very true. He seemed more open minded when we were just dating. Never showed any signs of this kind of attitude before." Zarifah's forehead crinkled. "I had no idea he would change like he has. He couldn't seem to understand that I have commitments. That I'd agreed to do shows, and I'm on troupe contract. I can't just drop everything, because he snaps his fingers, and says right now." She shook her head. "And I can't marry a man who expects me to jump, just because he says jump."

"No, you can't." Amina shook her head, along with Zarifah, agreeing with her. "Wives are partners, not trained dogs."

Zarifah continued with her story, telling it for the first time, to a good friend. "So I knew I couldn't marry him. That was the conclusion I came to, about us, and I told him the next night, after he still wouldn't see reason and change his mind about my dancing. When there was no talking it out, I said, 'I can't do this any more. You won't listen to me, or discuss this reasonably. I can't marry you.' I called the engagement off."

"Well, you had no other choice. It's a good thing you called it off, before you were married," Amina said.

Zarifah remembered how she'd held out the ring to Hassan, to give it back, but he hadn't taken it.

He wouldn't even look at the ring.

"I took the ring off to hand it to him, but he wouldn't take it," she said.

"Oh no." Amina's tone held dread for what was likely coming next in Zarifah's tale.

"He said, 'You're just nervous. It will pass. Brides get nervous. You are my betrothed. My perfect jewel. I have been searching for you for years, and now that I have found you, I will never let you go'," Zarifah said.

Amina's eyes widened. "Never let you go. Oh that does *not* sound good. Not when you are calling things off, and *want* him to let you go."

"I was in shock. Speechless. I just stood there with my hand out," Zarifah paused, shaking her head. "He ignored my hand, the ring, my shocked expression, and he acted as if everything was normal. Then he kissed my cheek goodbye, told me to get some sleep, that I'd feel better in the morning, and he was out the door, before I could even think what to do next."

"Wow." Amina sat back in her chair, as if she too was shocked.

"It was as if he didn't see me, or hear me, beyond the role he wants me to be in. I didn't know what to do. He hurried out the door, and I was sort of stunned."

"Sort of? That would shake any woman. Especially after pulling a Jekyll and Hyde switch you weren't prepared for. Of course he took you by surprise."

"Maybe he's never seen me. I mean really seen me." Zarifah shook her head. "Maybe he never saw past the dancer, to see the real me."

"I think you are right," Amina said. "He sounds like one of those who wants the dream, not the real woman. He sees Zarifah, the dancer, his beautiful dream girl. Not Edith, the woman behind that image."

*This was true.*

Zarifah was her dance name. Dance was only a part of who she was. But it was a part that she loved, and which brought her joy.

He saw no problem with her dropping everything, and just walking away.

She would never do that. Besides being their troupe director, Amina was her friend. The other dancers were her friends. But even if they hadn't been, she wouldn't go back on her promises and her commitments. She wasn't that kind of person.

This major problem between them, which had made her step back to take a closer look at him, and where things were headed, had changed her mind completely about marrying him.

She was an American belly dancer, with American sensibilities, living in the United States of America. Freedom was on an upper rung of the ladder of importance in her life. She could never marry a man who thought he could order her about, as if he owned her.

"Did he want you to give up teaching gymnastics too?" Amina asked. "Or just dance?"

"He didn't pay much attention to me teaching gymnastics," Zarifah said.

"No? But that's your job, and also very much a part of you."

"True." Zarifah nodded.

It was very much a part of her, more than her dance persona.

Edith Smith was her real name, and the one everyone associated with gymnastics. Trained from a young age, she had competed with an eye on Olympic gold, until she began to sprout up, taller than the other girls her age, her arms and legs growing so fast and awkward, in just one summer.

The tallest girl in her elementary school class, Edith felt gangly and awkward, not graceful. She would grow tall, and be more suited to basketball, than gymnastics. That's what her coaches had told her, as they'd turned their attention to younger, shorter girls, while dashing cold water on her dreams.

Now she taught gymnastics to children, and was much kinder to them than her coaches had ever been to her.

Belly dancing was a fun hobby on the side.

Belly dancing was freedom.

Dancing, she competed with no one, while her gymnastics background gave her a unique style of dance, as the other dancers were not as flexible as she.

"It sounds as if you really didn't know him either," Amina said. "He didn't show you his true colors, until now. And he didn't want to know the real you. Marriage to him would've been a major disaster."

"Yes, it would have," Zarifah agreed.

Dancing was where she felt most free. And she would never have given it up for Hassan.

She'd kept her dancing separate, using her dance name in public, and few people connected the two sides of her life, unless they were close enough to her for her to tell them.

Hassan had fallen for the dancer side. He'd been completely uninterested in the other side. He'd never seen her at work, never wanted to hear about it. She taught small children, that's all he cared to know. All he'd said after he'd asked her what she did for a living was, "Good. That means you will be a good mother, when you have children of your own."

They hadn't discussed whether she wanted to have children or not. She wouldn't mind having one or two, but it certainly wasn't what drove her. She had a career and a hobby, and both took large chunks of her time. She'd been too focused on building her business to even think about having children of her own, and she loved what she did.

*The driven, competitive, athletic side of a woman who'd nearly gone to the Olympics as a child, that strong, female businesswoman wasn't what Hassan wanted. He wanted a woman he could control.*

Zarifah could not be anything but what she was. Nor did she want to. She was very much a gymnast, and she loved to dance with her troupe. If he couldn't love her for who she was, she knew she had to call the engagement off.

Amina had been silent, listening, but now she spoke again. "So he walked out, leaving you holding that beautiful one-karat diamond ring with two rubies. Then what happened?"

"I overnighted the ring to him the next day, so he'd have to sign for it and accept it."

"Good. Smart lady." Amina nodded.

"I couldn't keep it. I don't want anything he gave me. But listen to this," she pulled her cell phone out of her bag and hit play.

Hassan's angry voice message played. "Zarifah, you do not throw my gifts back in my face with your messenger. You do not send your messenger to me, making me sign. I do not accept this. We are still engaged. You do not treat me like this!" His voice rose with each sentence as he became angrier.

"Oh no!" Amina had a horrified look on her face.

"He kept calling my phone, but I started deleting his messages, after this one, and didn't listen to any more of them. Then it got real quiet, and I thought he was done." She took a sip of tea, and swallowed, for her throat had gone dry with what she had to tell next.

Amina said, "Oh no," and patiently waited for Zarifah to go on.

Zarifah took a deep breath and continued. "He showed up at my apartment, and somehow got in. There's no sign of breaking and entering, and I could've sworn I locked the door. I *always* lock the door. But he came in, some way. He had the ring, and insisted I put it back on." She paused, frowning, remembering.

"Did you put it on?" Amina asked.

# Chapter Two

"No." Zarifah shook her head. "I refused. The rest is a blur. After I refused him, he got even angrier. He was very angry. It, well, it escalated. He started pulling my hair, so I couldn't move away, and he started hitting me."

Her eyes gazed off, away from Amina, as she relived the events in her mind.

Hassan had grabbed her ponytail, pulling her close. His brute strength was too much for her long slender arms, more used to dance and gymnastic flips, than to fighting.

She'd never had to fight anyone before, had never hit anyone, so she didn't know how to fight. She'd tried to pull away from him, but his grip only tightened. The more she struggled, the harder and meaner he'd fought, hitting her.

It was her screams that had brought a neighbor pounding on the door, calling out to her to answer, asking if she was all right.

Lost in her memories of that night, and losing her story telling ability, she stopped telling her story, and looked down at her tea.

*How do you explain what happened to you, when someone you loved, who was supposed to love you, turned into a monster, and started hitting you without stopping?*

Amina's hand closed over hers. "I understand. You don't have to tell me the rest, if you don't feel like it. I understand."

It was her kindness that allowed Zarifah to break through. The same way she pushed through with gymnastics training when she was bruised, and aching, and tired.

She told the rest of the story quick and flat, without emotion, to push through to the end.

That neighbor had called the police.

Luckily they had a patrol car just around the corner, and the police had arrived at her apartment complex within minutes.

Hassan hadn't stopped hurting her, until the police showed up, shouted 'Police!' and then kicked in the door, breaking in, and pulling him off her, taking him down, putting him in handcuffs to take him away.

He'd been charged and put behind bars. Now she had a restraining order as well.

"Oh honey," Amina squeezed her hand. "I'm so glad you're safe now. I'm so glad the police came in time to stop him and take him away." She held Zarifah's hand briefly, until Zarifah pulled her hand back, no longer needing the comfort.

She was usually quite independent. She didn't want to be pitied.

"I'm all right," she said. "The police came in time. He went to jail. I've pressed charges." She picked up her phone again, and hit the delete button on her phone messages. "I gave this to the police. I don't need to hear it again. Or read his texts. They have copies of those too." She looked up at

Amina, who had tears of sympathy in her eyes. "I have a restraining order on him now. He won't be allowed to come near me again."

"I'm glad. And I'm so glad you're all right." Amina paused, peering at Zarifah closer. "You're sure you're all right?"

"Thank you." Zarifah nodded. "Yes. I'm sure. I talked to a counselor this morning, and she pointed me in the right direction."

"That's good." Amina nodded. "Do you feel up to dancing tonight? Or are you ready to go home?"

"Yes, I want to dance, and I *need* to dance. It helps to dance things out," Zarifah said.

"It does." Amina smiled. "I know how that can be. Is it all right if I stay and watch?"

"Don't you need to get home to the kids?"

Amina had three children, under the age of ten, at home. Remembering how Hassan had said she ought to be home with her children, not running a dance studio, Zarifah pushed the thoughts and memories of him out of her mind. They'd crept in, and she wasn't going to allow that any more.

"Not tonight, I don't." Amina said. "Grant has taken them to visit his mother, and he can put them to bed after they get home."

"Okay. Then stay and keep me company," Zarifah said. "I'd like that. You can critique, and point out all my flaws."

Amina just smiled and poured herself more tea.

Zarifah rose and then, taking her veil out of her bag, she set her music to play and began to move, ignoring the stiffness and pain as she warmed up, moving through her dance solo.

Moving through the movements, stiff parts of her body

loosened, parts she'd been keeping still, after she'd been hit. Moving through the air with her veil, changing the dance, instead of sticking to her choreography, she added gymnastics moves as familiar to her as sleep. Moves that were strong and sure, movements as natural to her as breathing. Even the aching parts felt good, while somewhere deep in her soul, something released that needed to be let fly, something that spoke of freedom in body and in spirit. Caught up in the music and the dance, she forgot Amina was there, watching. She danced until she danced the memories out, along with the pain.

When she was done, she stopped; breathing hard, and then finally remembered her friend, who was still sitting in the chair, watching while silently sipping her tea.

"Perfect," Amina said, tears shining in her eyes. "Beautiful and perfect."

On a different day, Zarifah might have argued with her. She rarely thought of anything she did as perfect, and was good at finding flaws in herself, an attitude carrying over from her challenging childhood.

But tonight, she simply let those loving words from her friend sink in, soothing her, and sent her a soft smile with two soft words. "Thank you."

They collected their things, and started shutting down the studio for the night.

"There was something I'd wanted to talk to you about tonight," Amina said. "But then I wasn't sure if tonight was the time. I think now it is."

"What is it?" Zarifah asked, her curiosity now fully piqued.

"Have you seen the post about Shimmy Mob on the internet?" Amina's brown eyes shone with excitement as she pulled her long brown hair into a ponytail.

"No." Zarifah shook her head, her long black hair brushing her bare shoulders. "What's Shimmy Mob?" She reached in her bag for a big hair clip to pile her own hair up.

"It's an event to be held in May, on international belly dance day, all around the world. Everyone will dance to the same song, doing the same choreography, and there's a Shimmy Mob t-shirt everyone will wear. Each city team who signs up, will be raising funds for our local domestic abuse shelters." Amina's excitement could be contagious, and today was no exception.

"That sounds fantastic. But I've never heard of it before." Zarifah wanted more information before she committed to this project. "And you say it's all over the world?"

"No one has heard of it before," Amina laughed. "Because this is the first year for it. It is brand new!"

"How cool!" Zarifah was starting to catch the excitement, but then she caught herself. "Wait. You said 'our'. Does that mean we are doing this Shimmy Mob?"

"Yes! I just signed our city up, and agreed to be team leader. Dancers will sign up to dance. It's less than fifty dollars, and you get the music, the dance moves, a hip scarf and a t-shirt. So, let's do this!"

"I'm in. Sounds like fun, and all for a good cause!"

"Great! Amina's smile spread even wider. "Will you be my assistant?"

"Sure." Zarifah nodded.

"This is going to be awesome. It will help lots of women and children," Amina said.

Zarifah nodded again, and her thoughts drifted back to the night Hassan hit her. "I hope we raise a lot of money, and can help as many women and children as possible."

"I do too," Amina said. "And we will!"

As they headed outside, both excited about the upcoming Shimmy Mob, Zarifah reached into her purse for her new key ring with the pink pepper spray tube.

"Oh how cute. Is that a lipstick case?" Amina asked.

"No," Zarifah smiled. "It's my pepper spray."

"Oh!" Amina's face showed her surprise, and then she smiled too. "That is a great idea, to carry one of those."

"I just bought it today," Zarifah said. She peered into the darkness, hoping her ex-fiancé was still in jail, and not outside in the dark, waiting. She held the pink tube on her key ring, ready to spray anyone who came at her. She looked over both tense shoulders, heart racing.

"I'm glad the police took him away," Amina said, her calm voice helping to settle Zarifah's nerves, centering her in the present.

*No one is waiting to jump out at me. Good.*

But she couldn't help the feeling that Hassan would come back, angrier than ever, and hurt her again.

"I know you're nervous, honey, but he's behind bars now," Amina said.

"He will have made bail," Zarifah said. "He has plenty of money, remember? He could be out now."

"I'll watch you walk to your car, from now on," Amina promised. "We will all look out for you. And I'll have security at the show notified, and will show them his picture. Do you have a photo of him I could use?"

"No, I burnt them all, and deleted them off my phone. I blocked him on social media. I was so upset; I didn't think to save one photo to show anyone. I just wanted to never have to see him again."

"Well, if he is on social media, then I can find a picture of him. Call or text me, when you get home safe, okay?"

"Okay," Zarifah said.

"Thank you," Amina said.

Amina gave her a quick hug, and then they hurried to their cars.

Zarifah unlocked her car door, climbed in, closed the door, and then locked it right away. Only then did she exhale some of the tension she'd carried with her through the parking lot.

Maybe now that she'd had tea with Amina, and told her everything, she would be able to eat dinner. It had been a long day, and she was tired and suddenly quite hungry.

She could never eat before dance practice, so her dinners were often quite late, and her appetite quite large. But she hadn't felt much like eating since Hassan had attacked her.

Now it seemed her appetite was back.

* * *

Cutter stood inside the wedding chapel, taking it all in. The chapel was fully decorated with deep red flowers, delicate white baby's breath flowers, and dark blue ribbons. Against the dark wood of the chapel, it was tastefully elegant, and yet overflowing. Cutter had never seen anything like it. It was both patriotic, and very romantic and wedding like.

Christie worked at Floral Blessings Floral shop, and the owner, Mrs. Brown, who was sitting in the pew where Christie's mother and grandmothers would have sat, was the closest to family of anyone in Christie's life. The gray haired woman loved her like a grandmother. So, she'd done all the floral decorations as a gift, and they were stunning.

Cutter approved.

His grandfather had run a small nursery, and his grandmother loved flowers, so Tony had grown up with knowledge of them. Something he rarely talked about. Like a lot of things. He would however, make a point of letting the older woman know that the flowers were well selected, and well done. And he'd tell his grandmother about them. She would approve of the flowers. She would not approve of his date.

He glanced at Tawny, who cleaned up quite nicely, in a little black dress that showed off her curves. No one but he, knew she was wearing absolutely nothing beneath it.

She'd told him, the minute he'd picked her up, so she could tease him with it all evening.

For now, he had to keep his attention on his duties, as part of the wedding party. He was paired up with Lorrie, the hairdresser who'd done Christie's hair for the occasion. A thin white ribbon was part of that hairdo.

Lorrie saw him looking, and whispered, "Christi's garter is made from that ribbon. With a red bow added. I dare you to catch it."

He gave a brief shake of his head. No way was he catching any garter, or letting anyone think he'd be the next man to get married. That wasn't part of his immediate future game plan. And though he was a leg man, he really didn't need to watch his buddy's new wife hike up her dress, to show off her legs. Throwing the garter was one tradition that should've been done away with by now. It reminded him of stripping, and that made him think of sex.

Cutter liked women. A lot. And he dated lots of women. But he was particular about certain things. He was clear and up front about what he wanted. One reason he liked dating strippers, was that they could be up clear and up front too, and were usually sexually uninhibited.

Sex was never a problem for a SEAL.

Finding the perfect wife? That could be a problem.

R.T. had gotten lucky in that movie theater. Today, he looked like the luckiest man on the planet. Christie was a keeper. One look at the two of them, and you could see this was true love.

That's what Cutter wanted when he did marry. He wouldn't settle for anything else.

The ceremony was soon over, and pictures of the wedding party were next.

Tawny, who'd been waiting for him in the back of the church, slid her hand onto his arm when they were done with photos, and whispered, "I want a word in private with you. Don't let anyone see us."

*Stealth? Oh yeah. I can do stealth.*

He held back in the hallway, and then turned them toward a small room. "Go ahead," he called to Osprey. "We'll catch up with you at the reception."

Osprey nodded, watching Tawny.

Cutter gave him a short shrug, and then Osprey walked away.

Pulling his hand, Tawny tugged him into the empty room, and then hiked up her dress, showing him her bare body below her waist. "Let's do it here," she said.

"In the church?" he said.

*She's a wild one. Not one to take home to grandma.*

"Sure," she said, pulling her dress up enough to expose her breasts, which popped out with a bounce.

Despite his immediate reaction to the sight of her, he was not going to do it with her in the church. That seemed more than a little disrespectful.

"You know you like it," she said, and she wiggled her ass, which made her breasts bounce. "I'll be ready to go, any time. Keep that in mind, big guy. Weddings make me horny. Let's do it."

"Later," he said. "We've got to head to the reception."

She pouted. "Not even a quickie?"

He shook his head no, not amused by her little girl pout.

"Then find us a spot on the way," she said.

He pulled her dress down. "Later, Tawny. We've got to go."

Her pout grew bigger.

Losing his patience with her, he turned to head for the door.

As he'd expected, she hurried to follow him.

"Okay, okay, we can do it at the reception," she said. "Find us a spot."

He didn't respond to that, he simply said, "Come on."

She stopped pestering him about it, and grabbed hold of his left bicep. "I love your muscles." She squeezed his arm. "They feel so good."

None of this was having the affect she likely intended, as it had become very clear that Tawny was not the right woman. She was a 'for right now' kind of woman, and at this point he wasn't even sure about the "for right now" part.

They reached the reception, and Tawny was once again polite, and nice to everyone, with her sexual vibe tuned away down.

But for Tony, it was too late. He wasn't ready for sex at the reception. He wasn't ready for sex with her anywhere. He'd finish the date this evening, and then he was done.

Osprey and several of the other members of the team had eyed him, when he walked in, but nobody said anything to them about being the last ones to arrive. They hadn't been late.

Through the dinner and the toasts, everyone laughed and had a good time.

To Cutter, it was a visual delight, with many of the

women in the retro theme, which included the ladies in wedding party with their dresses, and even some of the guests.

When the time came for the garter toss, Cutter reluctantly got in with the group, but toward the back.

He watched as R.T. slid that garter off his new bride's leg to a saucy tune and whistled, as she blushed becomingly.

*Yeah, she's hot.*

He did not want to get turned on by his buddy's girl. That would not be cool.

He caught Tawny's gaze.

She winked at him.

Then the toss was up, and the single SEALs, and other single guys were shouldering each other, some trying to get the garter, some trying to avoid it, and others trying to push their buddy to get the garter.

It was up, it was down, it bounced off one guy's hand, who maybe didn't want it, and then fell down into the crowd of men, which made them look down for it, as if they were looking for a rugby ball amidst all the pushing and yelling.

*Crap it's on my leg!*

Lifting his knee he attempted to soccer knee punch it up, toward someone else.

*Not going to touch that thing.*

One of the other guys grabbed it.

*Whew. At least that's over.*

Tawny had watched the whole thing with a smirk.

He was fairly certain she didn't want to marry anyone either.

She was taking a class during the day, and stripped at night to pay her bills. She claimed to love stripping.

He watched her run her tongue around her red lips, a signal that she wanted him, right here, right now.

*Damn*

He headed for the bar, needing a drink.

"I can see why you didn't want to catch the garter, with that one watching," Kik said to him, low enough no one else could hear, as they waited for drinks. "You know she's dated SEALs before. Before you came onto the team, there was a big stink over her. Bar fights, slashed tires. It got real ugly. She'll fuck any guy who's earned a trident. Sometimes in the same night."

"Damn," Cutter said.

"Yeah," Kik said. "Just thought I'd warn ya."

"Thanks bro," Cutter said.

"Always got your six," he slapped Cutter on the back.

Cutter wondered who all she'd slept with. Suddenly any desire to sleep with her again withered. He was done.

He went up to Kik again. "So, which ones?"

"What?" Kik asked.

"Which SEALs?"

"Amigo, you really want to know?"

# Chapter Three

"Yeah." Cutter said. "I want to know."

"Trevor, Bales, and Magnum, Team two. Oscar and Buzz," Kik said.

"Our guys?"

Kik nodded.

Oscar and Buzz were on SEAL Team twelve, but they weren't at the reception.

"Our guys fought?" Cutter wanted to know what happened, and why none of his team had said anything to him about her before.

"Fought back," Kik said. "They didn't start it. But none of them will touch her now. Field is clear, if you want her."

Cutter grunted.

"That wasn't a happy sound, bro," Kik said. "Woman trouble?"

"Nah. I'm done after tonight."

"Smart," Kik said.

"How come none of you told me about her?"

"Didn't know you were still seeing her," Kik said. "Figured after the show was a one-night deal. She don't stick with anyone long, bro."

Diesel and Pippa's two beautiful children were running around laughing and ran past them, followed by their dad.

Bryce at three years, and Julie at one year, were both pretty darn cute.

Cutter glanced over at their mother, who was talking with Christie and laughing.

Christie and Pippa were two beautiful women.

He glanced at Tawny. Eyeing her and the other women, and wondering how many other SEAL's Tawny had been with, made her now appear less attractive.

She couldn't match the inner beauty of the two women, which shone through everything they did, and said.

Tawny was down and dirty sex. With everyone apparently.

Christie and Pippa were the take home to meet mama, or in his case, grandma type of women.

*Tawny was fast and exciting. Does she use sex to reel men in? If so, she's good at it. And she's fun. But there were other ways of having fun.*

The way Diesel and Pippa carried on, the two of them were still having fun, after being married a few years, and having two kids.

RT and Christie certainly were, as newlyweds.

*Maybe dating a good girl could be fun too, if you found the right one.*

The thing was, he'd gotten used to having fun with wild girls, and wasn't sure how to find one of those good girls.

*They wouldn't be hanging out in strip clubs.*

He needed to stop getting distracted by all the long-legged dancers in the clubs.

Sitting back down at their table, he reached for his glass of bourbon, and finished it off.

"Did you find us a place yet?" Tawny asked low, her hand moving beneath the tablecloth to his thigh, her fingers caressing his muscle. "I need you. Watching all those sexy men, jumping for that garter, really turned me on."

"Some women find SEALs really hot," he said.

"Hot blooded women," she whispered in his ear, and then flicked it with her tongue as her hand kept searching. When she found what she was looking for, her hand squeezed.

Then she released him and sat back with a smirk. Her eyes watched him, like a cat watching a mouse, before she glanced around the room, cool as if nothing had just happened.

His mind was on what she'd just done, and what she might do for him now, if he wanted her to and now, he couldn't stand up and move away from the table, without anyone noticing his reaction to her.

He needed another drink. He handed Tawny his empty glass. "This SEAL is overheated. Get me a drink."

"Just the way I like you." She grinned. "Hot, over-heated, thirsty, and bossy." She stood, and carrying the glass, walked toward the bar.

Diesel moved into her vacated seat. "I don't need to guess where you picked her up."

Cutter shrugged. "Yeah, she gave me her number at the club, so I called her after the party, and she came by my place after work."

"I should've warned you about her," Diesel said.

"Kik just did." Cutter shrugged. "It is what it is."

"You ever dated a woman who wasn't a stripper?"

"Sure," Cutter said. "Plenty of girls."

"Since you became a SEAL," Diesel said.

"Nope." Cutter shook his head.

"I sense there's a reason," Diesel said.

"I had a steady gir,l when I was in training. We lasted until the week I graduated and earned my trident. She broke up with me the day before, and she didn't even attend the ceremony. She had a new boyfriend. One who could take her to the movies every weekend, not one she had to wait for."

"Damn," Diesel said. "So, she broke your heart."

"I'm over it." Cutter shrugged. "Good girls deserve attention. I get that."

"Yeah, it can be hard on them," Diesel said.

Both of them knew the odds on marriages with SEAL team members. Many didn't stick together, and those that did, often had problems.

Diesel and RT were lucky, and they knew it.

"We've worked hard on our relationship," Diesel said. "You don't see it, because we don't talk about it. We've even gone to marriage counseling, to get some things straightened out, to be able to communicate better."

"Wow. I'd never have guessed."

"Well, the night we met, we were both wearing masks, we didn't know each other's names, and though we'd had great sex, we hadn't talked much. Add in a couple years, and the son we share together, and we were starting from a very unusual position."

"Yeah, I can see that." Cutter nodded.

"But everything is great, now," Diesel said.

"That's good to hear, man," Cutter said. "Maybe one day I'll have that too. Kids, a house, and a dog. The whole deal."

"First thing to do, is stop dating strippers," Diesel said.

"How about you try something else for a change? Pippa got tickets to an Arabian nights belly dance show next weekend. A friend gifted her with three tickets, but we're not taking Bryce. Three is too young to sit still through all that, and Pippa needs a night out, away from the kids."

"Yeah, I'd like to go, but are you sure Pippa wants you to invite me, instead of one of her girlfriends?" Cutter said.

"Yes, she just told me to come over here to ask you."

"Cool, then yeah, sure. Sounds like fun. The only belly dancer I've seen was at a strip club. She was hot."

"No way, bro." Diesel shook his head. "Pippa has informed me, that real belly dancers never take off their clothes. Those girls are just strippers wearing another stripper costume, with Velcro to play that character."

"Got it." Cutter nodded, just as Tawny walked back, with his drink.

"Here you go," she sat the drink in front of him.

"I'll get back to my table," Diesel said. "Chat with you later."

Cutter gave him a thumbs up.

When the dancing started, Tawny wanted to dance, so the minute the floor opened up to everyone, they headed to the dance floor. He knew she'd be a good dancer, and she was surprised at how good of a dancer he was.

Soon the floor was full of SEALs dancing with their wives and their girlfriends.

As the evening went on, Cutter realized that not only did Tawny like to dance; she was ready to dance with every guy there. He went to the bar for a drink, and she kept dancing. Not that he cared. He'd already decided this was their last date.

That nice little old lady, Mrs. Brown, who'd done the

flowers, was sitting alone, smiling with tears in her eyes as she watched the dancers.

He walked up to her table and pulled out a chair to sit next to her.

"Quite a party, isn't it?" he said.

"It surely is," she said. "My Jeff and I, we used to really cut a rug." She dabbed at her eyes and then smiled at him, before putting her embroidered handkerchief away. "He passed several years ago."

"Mrs. Brown, I'm Cutter," he said, "Though my grand-mother calls me Tony. Just don't use that one around the guys."

"It's nice to meet you, Tony," she said. "Thank you for sitting here with me. I was falling into sadness, missing my Jeff."

"Any time, Mrs. Brown," he said. "I wanted to compliment you on the beautiful floral arrangements you designed. They're stunning."

"Why thank you." She beamed at him.

He noted how her face, now lit with happiness, was looking years younger than when she'd been sitting there with sadness creeping in. It made his heart happy to cheer her.

"Here's something the guys don't know about me." Cutter said. "My grandfather used to run a nursery, and they delivered to flower shops in several counties. It was quite a thriving business in its day, before he passed. I used to follow him around, helping, when I was a small boy. So I know a few things about flowers. I know you chose some very expensive, high quality roses for the arrangements, and you put a lot of love into them."

She'd sat listening to him, her happiness growing with each word. "Well, I love Christie like a daughter, you see.

So she had to have the very best. She trusted me to surprise her. It's my wedding gift to her."

Being that Christie worked in the Floral Blessings Flower Shop with Mrs. Brown, she would know the value of the flowers, and the care that went into the display as well.

"I'm sure it touched her heart in a way that will be with her all her life," Cutter said.

"Thank you for your kind words," she said. "There's more to you than handsome, and strong." She tipped her head, and asked, "How does such a caring young man end up with such an uncaring woman?" She glanced over to Tawny, who was dancing with yet another SEAL, this time grinding her body in a dirty dance. "She's not behaving honorably toward you. Though you have toward her. You've been a gentleman."

"Well she's a stripper," he said. "Not my girlfriend. She's just my date for this evening."

"Usually it's the girls who settle," she said. "I see it all the time." She paused, and looked down at the wedding napkin, with the date and the name of the couple in silver across the top.

He knew she was implying that he was settling, instead of finding a good woman to marry. She and his grandmother would get along well.

"This one will last," she said. "I've been to many weddings, and can predict them well. It will last, because he is a high value male, and she is a high value female. And it will last, because they value each other, and don't pull on each other's value, bringing it down. That is the recipe for a long and happy marriage."

"I hope it lasts. They seem very happy," he said.

"It will," she said. "And you, young man, you just have

to find your high value female. And then value each other, and lift each other up."

"I'm not quite sure where to find her," he said.

"Just like flowers," she said. "Look for the fields where high value flowers grow."

Watching Tawny embarrass herself on the dance floor, as she got drunker, Cutter decided he'd better go see if he could salvage the situation. The happy couple didn't need any scenes at their reception, and he was starting to suspect that Tawny not only liked SEALs, she liked them fighting over her.

"I'd best go see to my date," he said. "Thank you for your company, Mrs. Brown." He took her hand in his, and gave it a gentle squeeze. "I've enjoyed visiting with you."

"Thank you, Tony," she said. "You find that high value girl, you call me, and we'll send her some flowers. Start you off on the right foot with her. Young men have forgotten how to send flowers to girls these days, unless it's a holiday, or they are apologizing. Simple bouquets seem to be out of fashion. My Jeff, he brought me flowers every Friday night, on his way home from work. Little bouquets usually. But oh, so full of love."

Now he was feeling emotional, and blinking moisture away from his eyes. "Thank you Mrs. Brown. I think your Jeff sounds like a great man. Reminds me of my grandfather."

She patted his hand. "I see it in you too. You're a high value man, and don't you forget it. Especially when rescuing that date over there."

He laughed. "I will."

She stood up to go. "I'm heading on home now. These parties get wilder, the more they drink, and then they get louder. I've had about all the loud my tired ears can handle tonight. Enjoy the rest of your evening."

"You too, Mrs. Brown. You too."

She made her way to the door, and he moved toward the dance floor again.

Tawny had a drink in one hand, and her other on one man's chest as she danced around him. For the first time since Cutter had asked her back to his place, he regretted that he'd asked. Not just asked her to the wedding, but asked her to go anywhere.

"Hey big man," she said to him when she saw him. "You took too long finding us a place to get it on, and I'm too turned on to wait, while you talk to some old woman." She started to run her hand down the other man's torso toward his crotch.

"You're drunk, Tawny. Are you ready to go?" he asked. He'd take her home, to her home; do the right thing, since she was his date. Be the gentleman. Even though she wasn't acting like a lady.

"No, I'm not ready to go home. I told you I wanted you to find a place here, and do me."

"Not going to happen, Tawny," he said.

"Well, if you won't, he will," she said, her hand patting the man she couldn't keep her hands off. "Jeff's a Marine. He can finish what you can't."

"That so."

There was no point to tell her that he didn't want to finish. She was drunk, and starting to cause a scene.

Someone needed to have a talk with Tawny, about being a high value woman. She didn't value herself.

Then it hit him what Mrs. Brown was trying to tell him.

By bringing Tawny to the wedding, he wasn't valuing himself.

"Cutter. You don't cut nothing," Jeff said, his chest puffing out. "Tawny needs a real man. So, I'm cutting in."

It sounded like Tawny wasn't the only one who was drunk. This was not cool to be happening at his friend's wedding, and it was his fault for bringing her.

"Everything cool, bro?" Kik had come up behind Cutter, covering his six.

Cutter was not going to fight over Tawny. "Yeah, it's cool. She isn't ready to go home. I offered." He shrugged.

"I don't want to go home with him," Tawny said, "I want to be with Jeff."

"You want to be with Jeff," he said, confirming what she'd said.

"Yeah, you heard me," she smirked, running her hand down to Jeff's crotch.

"Then be with Jeff," he said with a shrug. "Our date is officially over."

Her jaw dropped. "Wait. What?" She appeared stunned he wasn't fighting for her.

"I said our date is officially over," he said, and then nodded at them. "You two have a good evening."

Kik clapped him on the back, and the two of them walked away together.

"You handled it. I wondered at first, if Christie and R.T. were going to have wedding memories of a brawl on the dance floor," Kik said.

"Naw, man. She's not worth it," Cutter said. "I gave her the chance to stop acting like a slut, and go home and sleep it off, but that's not what she wants. And I'm not going to put up with a brawl at our brother's wedding."

"You okay, bro?" Kik asked.

"More than okay. I'd rather hang with you guys anyway. She requires a lot of attention."

Kik laughed. "Yeah, I could see that. Hey, there's a new bet going around the base, that you haven't heard about."

"What's the bet?"

"The bet is, who she's gonna do here, and in what room. They say she's got a thing for going at it in all sorts of places. Closets and rooms in busy buildings, empty houses in new subdivisions when there are tours, that kind of thing."

"Yeah, she does," Cutter said.

Kik gave him a look. "So about that church..."

"Yeah, she would have. But I made her wait," Cutter said. "Then I decided I'm done with her for good."

"You're doing the right thing." Kik reached the table where Fen, Big Mac, Matt, and Diesel were hanging out. "I'd hate to have to explain to our commander, why one of our best guys is ruining his career, by hanging out with the wrong chick, in the wrong places."

Cutter pulled out a chair. "Hey," he said to the others. "What're you guys jawing about?"

"You," Big Mac said. "Was wondering when you'd get fed up with her."

"You've never brought one of your girls to any of our events," Fen said.

"Mostly, I've taken them back to my place, or theirs for the night," he said. "But I'm done with all that."

"Stay out of the strip clubs, son," Matt said. "They are your downfall."

Kik spoke up. "Not any more they aren't. He's done."

Cutter shot Kik a glance, and Kik nodded at him, backing him up. Letting him know he supported the new choices Cutter was making.

"Good to hear, bro," Diesel said. "Pippa and Christie will be happy to hear it. They asked me if we had to invite her to the barbecue on Memorial Day. I told them hell, no."

"Yeah, she was out of line tonight," Cutter said. "Don't worry, I'm not gonna bring her."

He'd known he could do better. He just hadn't tried. Because the last high value girl he'd gone with had nearly ripped out his heart.

*But was she a high value girl, or just a good girl? A high value woman would have waited. Would have come to my graduation.*

They'd both been younger back then. Enough years had gone past. He very much wanted a woman with whom he could share parts of himself that he'd kept quiet about.

Like his grandparents, the nursery, other experiences and interests he had. It had been nice talking about them with Mrs. Brown tonight.

Sex was great, but when you were done, it was nice to be able to talk about stuff, and just enjoy each other's company. That had been missing in his life for a very long time. He didn't want a woman who just saw him as a SEAL, and was only with him because she thought that it was hot to date a SEAL.

He had a new goal. To find a high value woman who would care about his heart, not just the hard body that housed it.

The rest of the evening he spent drinking with the guys, putting Tawny out of his mind, which it turned out, was quite easy.

# Chapter Four

Two nights after Zarifah had shared her story with Amina, she was with the troupe again, in rehearsals at the studio, getting ready for their Arabian Nights show.

Student dancers who weren't in the troupe, were in the studio as well, and would rehearse after the troupe was done.

Zariah noticed other dancers eyeing her arm. She'd put heavy stage makeup on tonight, and had covered the bruising on her face, hiding most of it. But the biggest bruise on her arm was highly visible. Makeup wasn't going to cover a bruise that purple.

She rubbed at it briefly.

"Does it hurt?" Amina asked with concern.

"A little. But mostly it's ugly." She looked down at it. "I should get some of that makeup that covers tattoos. The kind actors use. But I'm not sure what it's called, or where to find it."

"It will soon be healed, and no one will see it by

Shimmy Mob day," Amina put her arm around her. "There's time. It's one month away."

"I know. I just signed up last night," Zarifah said.

"That's great!" Amina's face lit up.

"One month isn't long to learn the dance," Zarifah said.

"It's not." Amina agreed. "But I only just found out about the event myself, and I signed us up as soon as I could."

"Well, we've learned other dances in less time." Zarifah shrugged. "So I guess I shouldn't worry. We can do it!"

"That's right, we have," Amina said. "And we'll all be learning the dance together. This event allows brand new dancers to join in, too, so we might be teaching some of them the moves. I'll probably need all of you to help the newer students learn one on one, since we don't have much time, depending on how new they are. It's hard for a brand-new dancer to learn from a video. They've got to learn the right posture."

"I remember my first class. You kept saying tuck your tailbone!" Zarifah laughed. "And I was a gymnast, so I didn't have posture problems. I remember what it was like to be new to this dance though, and I'll be happy to help the new students."

"Yes, you didn't need as much instruction as some," Amina said. "I'm so thankful for your help with Shimmy Mob and your help with teaching the new dancers. The first thing we have to do, is to get the word out to all the dancers in town, and ask them to sign up."

"Yes! Are you announcing it here, tonight?" Zarifah knew Amina hadn't told any of the troupe dancers about Shimmy Mob yet, and usually she told the troupe any news before she told the other dancers. This time she hadn't.

"Yes. I made up these fliers last night." Amina showed

her a stack of fliers. "Can you hand them out, while I make the announcement?"

"Sure." Zarifah reached for them.

"Thank you." Amina handed her the fliers and then clapped her hands. "All right ladies! Attention please."

One of the women made the high-pitched "lelelelelele" zaggahret sound, and the eight women all hushed immediately.

"I have some exciting news!" Amina began. "We are holding the first Shimmy Mob event in our city. How many of you have heard of Shimmy Mob?

No one raised their hands.

"Shimmy Mob raises awareness of domestic abuse, and raises funds for our local domestic abuse shelters. It is an international event taking place all around the world on International Belly Dance Day."

"I didn't know there was an international belly dance day," Bayda said. "How exciting!"

"There is," Amina said. "And we're going to show the world what we can do. We'll be dancing to the same song, doing the same Shimmy Mob choreography, and wearing the same Shimmy Mob T-shirts, along with our dance sisters all around the world." she smiled.

"I just got goose bumps," Farrah said. "This is so wonderful."

Zarifah could see them on Farrah's light brown skin. She'd worked for the Peace Corps in Thailand, and had met her extended family on her mother's side. Her dark eyes shone with excitement at the news of Shimmy Mob.

"I got them too," Zarifah said.

Farrah sent her a happy smile.

Zarifah waited for Amina's nod, to hand out the fliers. She was excited to be involved in this new project, and so glad she hadn't given up her dancing for Hassan. If she had, she would have missed this wonderful event, and sharing the experience with her dance sisters. Her thoughts moved away from him.

This event would unite their group with their dance sisters all around the world. And they would be helping women all around the world to escape from dangerous situations, like the one she'd been rescued from. It was more than exciting. She had goose bumps, and a good feeling about the event.

How close she had come to being married to Hassan. *What if he hadn't changed until after the wedding?*

She couldn't imagine what it would be like to live with a man like him. To be married to him. Horrible was one word that came to mind. Dangerous was another.

Too many women found themselves in dangerous situations. Now there was something she could do to help. They could all help.

"This is an important cause," Bayda said. "I'll do anything I can to help. I'm so glad we're doing this."

Amina nodded. "It is. I'm thankful for your help. I'm the team leader for the event, and Zarifah is my assistant team leader. One of the things we're supposed to do, is spread word about the shelter. Let women know what is out there for them in our area. Raising awareness for the shelter is one of our goals. But first, we need to know what those options are. Zarifah, can you research that info for me?"

"Sure. I'd be happy to. I already have a head start because the counselor I talked to gave me a brochure for one place."

"Excellent." Amina addressed the entire group again. "Ladies, I'm going to turn this over to Zarifah, so she can share her story with you. And she has fliers for you as well."

Zarifah started to hand out the fliers, and to talk about what had happened to her. When she was done, she realized her friend had given her something to keep her busy, while she talked, which had made it a bit easier to do the telling.

Now that she'd shared her story, she found that telling them had been easier than she'd thought.

The women's hugs, their tears, and their concern for her right now, told her how much these women cared. They were her dance sisters, soon to be her Shimmy Mob sisters.

Goose bumps covered her arms.

This seemed to be becoming a thing, getting goose bumps in connection with Shimmy Mob. It was pulling out her feelings in a deep way. She wondered if that was just her, or if any of the others were feeling it too.

Amina smiled. "Thank you, Zarifah." She turned to address the group again. "We have to get the music, and the choreography, and start practicing," she said. "Once you sign up as a dancer, and pay the fee, you'll get access to the website section for our team. The dance is on three videos there, broken down into three different dance styles."

"Three? Oh boy," Bayda said. "I only know one."

"Most dancers only know one," Amina said. "A few know two. So we're all learning at least one new style and moves. Parts one and three are Cabaret, and part two is ATS or American Tribal Style with Tribal Fusion. But don't worry. Everything is on the videos. The choreography is broken down so we can learn it a section at a time. Then there's a final video with the complete run through to the music. Once you've signed up, I'll set up a schedule for rehearsals."

She walked over to put music on for tonight's rehearsal.

"But now ladies, we have a show to get ready for, so we

need to get started on our rehearsals. Please remember to take a few extra fliers at the end, before you leave, and hand them out to invite all your dance friends to dance with us. Post them up where you can. Shimmy Mob welcomes beginning dancers."

The circle of dancers around Zarifah began to thin, as they moved back to where their starting places where.

Amina started the music, and dancers glided out into the middle of the studio floor to begin to dance.

Everything went smoothly, and then the student dancers collected their things before leaving. Only the eight troupe dancers remained. Amina, Zarifah, Farrah, Latifah, Bayda, Nasheeta, Saba and Isis.

Her closest dance sisters.

Troupe dancers could each teach, and could take on paid gigs when those came in. They often met separately to talk about troupe business, and met socially as they enjoyed each other's company.

Zarifah hadn't been taking any paid gigs, since starting to date Hassan, because to him, paid dancers were like prostitutes.

The moment he asked her, "You do not dance for pay?" with that look on his face, and she'd said, "No, I only dance for fun. I like the music, and dancing with the other women." The expression on his face had cleared. That was apparently acceptable to him.

She wished now, that she'd said, yes, instead.

One small lie, though she'd justified it to herself, by telling herself that from that moment on she didn't dance for pay, so it wasn't really lying, had set up their relationship on a path she should never have been on. Maybe, had she fully disclosed then, she'd have seen the real Hassan in the beginning.

Neither of them had been fully honest. So neither of them could realize they were not suited for each other.

She would never make that mistake again.

*One small lie, even a lie of omission, at the beginning of a relationship, is like building a house with a small hole in the foundation. All the pieces aren't there.*

If she ever decided she was ready to date again, she wanted to make sure neither of them left any of the pieces out.

Both men and women should be fully themselves when they were together. No veils between them, no acting, or playing games.

The next guy would have to be completely himself.

If she ever went out again. Something she wasn't sure about.

The guy had better be rock steady, all American, and never try to curb her independence.

* * *

Cutter had called things off with Tawny, and had already had to turn down her offers for a quickie three times in two days. He wondered if she was a nymphomaniac. Yeah, she was good at sex, but he needed more than that. Maybe he'd needed to meet a woman like Tawny, to make him more aware of that. His cell phone buzzed again and he looked down.

*Tawny.*

He wasn't going to answer her this time, and was done with being polite.

*No contact. That's the best practice for cutting off anyone who is so persistent. Because they take any response as encouragement.*

Likely some men would give in, if she tempted them enough.

But Cutter wasn't like most men. He'd proved that joining the SEAL team.

If she liked dating SEALs so much, then she ought to be used to this by now. He wasn't the only guy on the team with enough self-control to cut her off.

Once he did, he'd heard a few more stories.

She was trouble, once she got her hooks into a man.

He deleted her text message, and then called his grandmother.

When she answered the phone, he said, "Hey grandma. Thought I'd check in on you."

"Tony boy! I love hearing from you," she said. "You didn't forget your old grandmamma."

"Of course not, grandma. I could never forget you."

"They're not sending you across the pond again, are they? To that desert of vipers?"

"No. They're not sending me anywhere, yet. I thought I might come out and visit you. You know, before they do send me somewhere."

"I would love that," she said. "Will you be here for dinner?"

He laughed. She always asked him that, when he said he was coming over, and she loved to cook for him. Even in her eighties, she still loved to cook for the people she loved. "No, grandma, not that fast. I'll get my flight schedule, and tell you soon. Just had my leave approved, and wanted to give you the dates first."

"Oh that is good. Let me sharpen my pencil. The led just broke from so much excitement."

He heard the whirl of an electric pencil sharpener and

grinned. She was always breaking pencils because she pressed so hard.

Going to his grandmother's house was like stepping back in time with her old-fashioned utensils of all kinds. But she loved her electric pencil sharpener. Sometimes he wondered if she broke the pencil leads on purpose, just to use it, or if she really did press that hard every time she wrote.

"Now, it's sharp again, like you, my sharp grandson. Now, I'm ready."

"Okay grandma. I have a whole week. So I'll have plenty of days to visit with you, and to fix anything around the house that needs fixing."

"That's good. There are a few things."

"Make a list for me, so I can see it when I get there." She didn't know text, or write emails, but he could always count on her to write an old-fashioned handwritten letter. The letters were things he'd treasured over the years, and now filled a sock drawer in his bedroom, along with other mementos.

"Yes, I'll do that," she said.

He gave her the dates next, and then she told him about her day, the neighbors she'd talked to, what she'd bought at the grocer, what she was making for dinner. When she started in on the nice girl she wanted to introduce him to, he said, "Love you, grandma, but I've got to call the airlines now, and buy my ticket. I'll call you again tomorrow, after work."

She could sometimes be hard to get off the phone, but he knew it was just because she missed him, and was lonely. He knew what it was to be lonely. That was one reason he'd kept going out with strippers.

If he could have talked his grandmother into moving out

to be near him, he would have. But she was stubborn, and she loved the home she'd lived in for years, while her health was still good, and she got around.

He understood stubborn, it was where he'd gotten that trait from, more than likely. A family trait. One that had helped him to get through his training.

She still drove herself, in her old white Cadillac, which would likely be a collector's item one day. While he was there, he'd check on her car. He started making a list of his own, of things to fix while he was staying with her.

* * *

After rehearsals were over, Amina gathered the troupe dancers together in the corner and said. "Remember, we're supposed to meet an hour before the Arabian Nights show, to try on the new costumes that are coming in this week."

She turned to Zarifah. "You can update me on what you've learned about our Shimmy Mob dance site options then."

"Sounds good. What color did you order for me?" Zarifah asked.

"Red, of course," Amina said. "Like always."

Zarifah smiled. She did like red.

Everyone said it went with her long dark hair, and pale skin. The right shade of red would set off her blue eyes.

Eyes that Hassan had told her were prettier than the sea. He'd been full of complimentary words at first, before he'd flipped his switch, totally changing his way of treating her. He'd told her that she was his jewel.

She needed to stop thinking about him and his pretty words, and move on.

The Hassan she knew and had fallen for wasn't the real

man. She'd fallen for a dream, as he'd tricked her, and the dream wasn't the reality, so now the adjustment was something she was having trouble getting used to, for her heart wanted that dream man who didn't exist. Her mind and heart were still adjusting to that, and it was taking longer than she wished.

Focusing on the new costume was one way to move on. Getting rid of a few costumes that reminded her of him would be another.

"I have some costumes to sell," she said. "Can you put them on consignment for me?"

"Of course, honey." Amina smiled. "Which ones are you selling?"

"The white and gold dress, the black and silver dress, and the purple bra and belt with skirt. Put whatever price on them you think is best. I want them to sell."

Understanding filled Amina's eyes. The gold dress, Hassan had bought her, and the other two were favorites of his. All three outfits were expensively beaded and expensive. They were her showiest costumes. He had called her his princess Zarifah when she wore them. She didn't want to wear those outfits again.

"I want to buy your white and gold one," Bayda said. "It's hard to find costumes that go with my red hair."

"I'd rather not see them again, even on one of my dance sisters," Zarifah said. "Sorry, Bayda. Otherwise, I'd sell it to you right now."

"It's okay. I understand," Bayda said.

Amina said, "Time for a new start. If I list them online, they'll sell faster."

"Then that's what I want to do." Zarifah nodded.

"I understand. You've got it," Amina said. "Your new costume will be here, just in time for your new start."

"Did you get me the gold sequined costume, or the silver?" Zarifah asked.

"The gold," Amina said. "I thought that combination looked richer with the red, than the silver. And a red veil to match, instead of gold."

The show's theme this year was Arabian Nights, and they'd all been excited about it. But Zarifah was no longer enamored by Arabian things, though she knew the others were. She would never daydream about sheiks again.

What she needed was an American man who understood her. A knight who would fight for her, not one who would fight her and hit her, and hold her back.

She wondered if Hassan still had the Arabian Nights show ticket she'd given him, and if he'd try to attend the show. She hoped he didn't, but how could she stop him?

The show was open to the public, and anyone who had a ticket could get in. It was a theater Amina had rented to put on their show.

The troupe dancers had never had a problem at a show before, and this one didn't have security guards. For the first time, Zarifah wished they had. She'd have to ask Amina about it later. Maybe Amina would have an idea of someone they could get to be security for the show that night.

She was busy right now though, as they were getting ready to run through the troupe dances that would be performed at the show.

"Everyone ready?" Amina asked, as she took her place in the front of the room. "We need to run through Nile Streams again, and work on better synchronization after the entrance number. So I'm going to play the end of the first number, and we'll work on that transition."

Once everyone was ready, they began, and Zarifah

thought no more of Hassan, as she was swept up into the complicated dances, giving herself to them.

When she danced, she danced with her body, mind, and soul. It was a freer expression for her than gymnastics had ever been, and the thing she loved most about it.

She let the music pull her into that state of graceful Zen which dance gave her.

* * *

Zarifah looked up from her seat in the green room, where she was sitting, while Bayda applied gold glitter over Zarifah's eyelids to enhance her stage makeup. Her own hands had been shaking too much to apply it herself, as her tension around whether Hassan would use his ticket to come see the show had her twisted tight with nerves.

Amina had hired a bouncer to provide security at the event, and the man who'd just entered the green room was a big brute of a man.

But Zarifah wasn't frightened of him. Instead, she was glad Amina hadn't hired some skinny guy.

She knew Hassan's strength. It would take a big man to subdue him.

Hassan was the one she was afraid of.

The bouncer had been given a photo of Hassan, and he'd been watching the crowd fill the theater seats.

She looked up at him, holding her breath, waiting for what he had to say, afraid to ask him what she was thinking.

*Is Hassan here, in the audience?*

# Chapter Five

"No sign of him," the bouncer said. "I'll keep watching. Just wanted you to know, before you go on. Ease your mind."

*Hassan isn't here. Oh thank God.*

Her shoulders dropped down, as some of the tension released. Now maybe she could relax, and just dance. "That's very thoughtful of you," she said. "Thank you for letting me know."

"You're welcome," he said and stepped back out again, closing the door.

"A man of few words, and big muscles," Bayda said. Then she giggled. "Real big muscles."

"It was nice of him to come and tell me that," Zarifah said. "Very thoughtful."

"He's all business, too," Bayda said. "Isn't that sexy?"

"I'm not looking for a sexy man," Zarifah said. "I'm going to stick to teaching gymnastics and dance. And just be happy being me. Since men can't seem to handle all of me."

"Because you are just so much awesome in one package," Bayda said. "Few men can handle that. Only a very special man will be able to handle so much awesome."

Zarifah laughed. "If you say so."

"It's good to see you more relaxed." Amina said. "Everything is going to be fine."

"Well, I do say so," Bayda continued, "You're awesome, and we all know it. Men are stupid." She reached into her bag. "Here, try this new perfume I bought. It has jasmine, and tiare flower scents in a nice blend." Taking it out, she handed it to Zarifah.

Taking the perfume bottle, Zarifah spritzed her inner wrists, waved one in the air, and then the other to dry them faster, and then took a sniff. "Oh, that is nice," she said. "I'll have to get some of that. Thank you."

"You're welcome."

Amina said, "Okay ladies, it's show time!"

They heard the intro music starting. There would be two short musical numbers to prepare the audience to step into an Arabian Nights world.

The energy in the green room was up, the dancers ready to perform.

Zarifah stood and started rolling her shoulders, beginning to do small warm up moves, to get her body ready. She stood, moving her knees back and forth, fast, in the small movements of a shimmy freeze. The green room was crowded, so her movements were small, but this shimmy freeze she always did before she performed, was more than a warm up for her knees. It was also how she sent tension out of her body, before going on stage.

The excitement in the room was catching, and she felt it even more so than usual, now that she was worried.

Now if she could just stop worrying about him, and just dance. The flips she did, required her full attention, and a distraction of any kind wouldn't be good. That was the kind of thing that used to make her fall off the balance beam, missing a hand placement, because something outside of her threw her slightly off. She didn't want that kind of thing happening tonight, to ruin her dance.

She closed her eyes and shimmied faster, trying to visualize all her stress moving down through her knees, down her legs and feet, and into the floor.

* * *

Cutter stepped into the theater, behind Diesel and Pippa, as they moved down the aisle, to their seats. Finding their row, they moved into it, found their seats, and then sat.

The lights dimmed, and music filled the air. Sweeping violins, and what sounded like a full orchestra, set the scene for a romantic Arabian night in the desert.

Not exactly the way Cutter remembered his time in the Middle East. For him, this show tonight would be total fantasy, like watching an Aladdin cartoon movie, or an old rerun of that show about an astronaut and a genie. Despite his time in the Middle East, he'd never seen a real belly dancer dance. Since, as Pippa had said, the stripper didn't count.

Many dancers came out for the opening number, and he enjoyed watching them. They weren't what he'd expected at all.

None of them looked Middle Eastern, but appeared like a cornucopia of many types of women, of varying skin color and hair color.

He'd barely glanced at the program before the show, noted all the Middle Eastern names, and how many dances there were, but that was all.

The program showed dance numbers alternating between the eight group dancers in the troupe, and dances where the troupe and student dancers performed together. In between those dances, were solos by each of the eight troupe dancers. The opening number and closing number contained all the dancers. Each dancer was named and the names were obviously dance names.

Zarifah would be the next number.

She entered to mysterious sounding music, with a red veil wrapped around her, even her head, so that Cutter couldn't see her fully, only that she wore a red and gold bra, a red and gold beaded belt with fringe, and a red skirt beneath the red veil, which she could see through, to her audience. Her eyes were lined with the dark kohl often seen on women in the Middle East, as they peered out from their veils.

The beginning moves of Zarifah's dance mimicked this, and the blue of her eyes and her pale skin struck him with how stunningly beautiful she was.

Then the music changed, and she burst out of her veil, her hands still holding it, and he saw her long dark hair, and the pale skin of her graceful arms and legs. Tall for a dancer, she glided, and then spun, using her veil, the veils movements as fascinating as the dancer herself.

Fascinated, Cutter took in her every move, every expression of her face. Her dance skill was amazing. He'd never seen anything like it.

She was beautiful, moving with both a dancer's grace, and with an athlete's power, in a way the other dancers hadn't.

He wondered what she did, along with her dancing, to give her that athleticism. Her movements alternated, some smooth and flowing, and some strong bursts of power. Her long dark hair flew out behind her, and her veil soared through the air.

She danced like a goddess. Like a queen. She had a majesty he couldn't have put into words, but he saw it, and felt it.

Her dance pulled him to her, as if she'd wrapped that veil around him, bringing them closer.

Then she bent over backward, her long arms touching the floor, one foot still on the floor as she went into the flip, the other leg coming up to go over, followed by the other leg. Her long slender legs fully visible, all the way up her legs to red dance panties, her pale skin beautiful against the red.

His breath caught. Those long sexy legs and her movements, along with the music, were the most erotic sight Cutter had ever seen. They reached out and called to him.

Smitten, he knew he had to meet her.

Cutter knew a thing or two about meeting dancers, and getting them to go out with him. This one was no stripper though, and he didn't know if she was single.

He would take a different approach, and treat her like a high value woman.

Taking out his phone, he pulled up Mrs. Brown's information, and placed an order, paying extra for quick service and delivery. Then he put his phone back down and continued watching the dancers, who while good, were nowhere, in his opinion, as good as Zarifah.

She was in a class all her own.

Intermission came and the house lights went up again, for a ten-minute intermission.

"Everything okay?" Pippa asked, gesturing to his phone.

"Yeah. I just had to order something," he said.

"Here? Now?" she asked, laughing. "I thought you had a thing for dancers."

"Yes." He nodded. "I do."

She just shook her head at him, and then the three of them went out to the lobby. They moved around looking at the colorful art on the walls, which was for sale.

He hoped Zarifa might step out of the green room briefly, but no dancers appeared.

Then, when intermission was almost over, they went back in and took their seats again.

The second half of the show was just as good as the first, and Cutter now looked for Zarifah every time the black curtains opened again. He thoroughly enjoyed her dancing. She was not only beautiful; she was mysterious, and intriguing.

When the show was over, there was a standing ovation, and then the director thanked everyone for coming.

Diesel's cell phone rang and he answered it. Their three-year-old son, Bryce was running a fever. After Diesel hung up, he said, "Hey man. Sorry to bail on you for drinks and snacks, but we need to get home to Bryce."

"No problem, bro." Cutter said. "I understand. I hope the little guy is better soon."

"Thanks," Diesel said. "Me too."

Everyone gave quick hugs, and then Diesel and Pippa were off, hurrying home.

Cutter wondered if the flowers he'd ordered had been delivered yet. He'd ordered half a dozen roses of varied colors, and some white baby's breath in a vase. Since he didn't know what her favorite flower was, or her favorite color.

Most men went for red roses, but Cutter had his own way of doing things. He knew the language of flowers, and wasn't sending any sort of message to a woman he hadn't met yet. Varied colors was safe and non-threatening and, with no undertone message attached to them, she could just enjoy the flowers.

Zarifah was in the green room, putting all her costumes into the suitcase she carried them around in, when a delivery person knocked on the door ,and asked for her by name.

Farrah who'd opened the door, pointed over to where Zarifah knelt, and the delivery person came in, carrying flowers.

"What in the world?" Zarifah said as she stood up. "Who is sending me flowers? I'm not even dating."

Hassan had always sent red roses; saying only red roses were good enough for a beautiful woman. So it wasn't him. And he would have sent twelve, or two sets of twelve, if he were feeling extravagantly generous, as he often was.

*This bouquet was beautiful.*

"I've never seen one like this," she said. "With all the colors."

"There's a card," Bayda said. "Open it."

Zarifah opened the card.

*Zarifah,*

*I enjoyed your dancing tonight. I hope you enjoy these flowers.*

*Cutter C.*

"I don't know anyone named Cutter," she said. "Does anyone here know a Cutter C.?"

All the dancers shook their heads and said, "no."

"Well, they're lovely," Amina said. "And your dance was too, so I'm not surprised you have a new admirer. Just enjoy them."

"Oh, I will," she said. The relief that Hassan hadn't showed up, and hadn't sent the flowers, made her relax again.

*It's going to be fine.*

"Does everyone have everything before we go?" Amina said. "Someone do a quick walk through, across the stage, to make sure nothing was dropped. The stage lights are still on, but I need to tell the lights and sound guy that he can go."

They collected all their things, and were carrying them out of the green room, when Zarifah saw a tall, handsome, dark haired man, dressed in black pants and a blue shirt, by the doors which led outside, waiting for someone.

Something about him felt familiar.

*How do I know him?*

They stepped closer to the door, and she got a better glimpse of him.

He had brown eyes and was smiling at her.

The smile warmed her from the inside out, as if he'd lit a candle.

*No, I don't know him. But it feels as if I do.*

Though she'd never seen him before.

Their security guy was waiting, to escort them to their cars. She hadn't even noticed him until now, and he was a big guy. Quite noticeable with his build. How had she missed seeing him? She'd been distracted by that handsome man.

*Oh, I do not need to get twitter pated about a man right now. Not with Hassan out there. I need to pay attention to my surroundings. Focus.*

"Miss Zarifah," the tall dark haired man said. "I enjoyed your dancing."

"Thank you," she replied, a warm blush spreading across her cheeks and neck.

*Why am I blushing? I'm used to people complimenting me on my dancing. Oh, but this man, he's more than hot.*

His voice reached something deep inside of her, and the way their eyes now met and connected, this was hormonal attraction on steroids. Something she'd never experienced.

Part of her wanted to pull her gaze away. Part of her wanted to stay.

"I hope you enjoy the flowers," he said.

"Oh, you sent them?" The surprise nearly knocked her over.

*He sent them? This handsome guy? Oh my.*

"Yes, I'm Cutter," he said.

"Nice to meet you, Cutter, and thank you for the flowers," she said.

"You're quite welcome," he said. "I'm glad you like them."

"It's an unusual arrangement, all the different colors. I've never seen one like this."

"My grandfather owned a nursery, so I know a few things about flowers. It's limiting to choose only one color, when there are so many variations."

*A man who understand flowers, and puts thought into floral selections,* she thought. *How fascinating. But, oh, is he gay? Maybe he's into dance shows and flowers because he's gay.*

That thought was tossing water on her attraction to him. But he was so hot. As was this attraction. Even the thought of him being gay wasn't putting it out.

*Oh, I hope he isn't gay.*

"You probably have guys asking you out all the time," he said. "Your dancing is sensual and enticing. But there's more to you than that."

Now every fiber in her being wanted to hear what he had to say next.

"You're an athlete," he said. "You move like an athlete. You've had training in something beyond dance."

*He sees me. He really sees me. All of me, not just the dancer. He sees past the performance. Oh God, I hope he's not gay. Please don't let him be gay.*

Because every part of her being wanted to, shout yes!

Their meeting seemed profound, fated. The way his voice, and his eyes, were making her feel, was like something out of a movie.

But she remained cautious. She had no idea what this was, or where it was going.

"Yes. I was a gymnast as a child," she answered.

"Still are, as far as I can see," he said. "You're very good. Where did you train?"

"I was at the ..."

Amina interrupted. "Our table at the restaurant is ready, and we're all starving."

Zarifah was as well, but she'd momentarily forgotten. The handsome man had captured her attention, and she didn't want the conversation to end yet.

"Cutter, if you'd like to continue our conversation, why don't you join us?"

Amina's eyebrows rose.

"I'd love to," he said.

"El Patron, two blocks from here," Zarifah said. "We're going for Mexican for tonight. None of us eat, before we dance, so we need to get over there, and order. If you'd like to meet us over there?"

"Perfect," he said, and smiled. "I'll see you there."

His smile made her break into a huge grin. "Yes, see you there."

Everyone headed to his or her cars, and this time,

Zarifah didn't look over her shoulders, to see if Hassan was anywhere waiting.

He hadn't come to the show, or tried to contact her lately, so it really must be over, and he'd likely moved on.

As Cutter went to his car, he was aware of their surroundings. Situational awareness at all times was a way of life for him, not something he turned on, and off. Being unaware could get you killed.

He noted a black Mercedes, in the back lot, next to the theater's parking lot, with a man inside who sat, talking on his phone. There were no other cars in that lot.

When they each pulled out of the theater parking lot, the man stayed in his car, on his phone and didn't follow them.

Cutter drove to the restaurant, excited to be getting to know the beautiful dancer a bit more. He parked, and then went in to join the group, still wondering who the man was, and if he'd been there watching someone, or waiting for someone.

With eight troupe dancers, and four companions, they were seated for twelve.

Cutter had a chair on the right side of the table, on the end. Not optimal, as he had his back to the door, and the chatter of so many women was high pitched and noisy, but at least he was across from Zarifah, and would have the chance to get to know her a little bit.

And she'd invited him into her world, something, which had surprised her director.

Once the drink orders and food orders were in, introductions went around the table, as he was a newcomer to their party.

Zarifah of course he'd met.

Amina, the troupe director, was there with her husband,

Thomas Ballantine, a slightly balding man, who looked like a businessman. Bayda, a slim, pale, redhead was by herself, and sat with the only blonde dancer, Saba, who was with her husband, Ken, a slim effeminate looking man. The two black dancers, Latifah and Nasheeta were cousins, though they didn't look like they were related at all. Latifah had a big bosom, and more curves than Nasheeta. And Isis, who appeared to be Chinese or Korean was with her husband.

Most of the dancers had changed into day clothes, but all still wore their heavier stage makeup, and a lot of jewelry, which jingled.

Already he was finding belly dancers much more interesting than strippers.

Zarifah out shone them all.

"I'm Cutter," he said. "Nice to meet everyone."

Pleasantries now exchanged, the drinks, chips, and salsa had arrived and everyone began to snack and drink.

He noted, as Zarifah was looking away from him, and dipping her nacho chip into her salsa, that she had a lot more makeup on one side of her face, which looked like it was covering some bruises. And when her wrap slipped off her arm and shoulder, that her arm was badly bruised. He wondered what had happened to her, but kept a poker face, and glanced away acting as if he hadn't noticed.

Taking charge of the table conversation, redirecting things, he said, "I'm curious. Your dance names are mostly Arabic, obviously stage names. How do you select them?"

Amirah answered him first. "The troupe name, Silk Lotus, was the name of my business, when I first started teaching yoga, and mediation. When I added belly dance, I kept the name, and we became the Silk Lotus dancers. But our style is for the most part, classic Egyptian, so we chose dance names to reflect that."

"Interesting," he said.

"What he's too polite to ask," Latifah said, "Is whether this is cultural appropriation."

"Mm hmm," Nasheeta nodded. "I know that's right."

"Obviously I'm Chinese," Isis spoke up. "I chose my name, because I love the Isis statues, and when I dance, I'm envisioning myself to be dancing the dance of Isis. The dancer chooses who the dancer wishes her dance to represent."

"Though it may seem like all of our names are made up," Farrah said. "Three of us are using our real names. Can you guess which ones?"

He grinned. He would guess, but was fairly sure of his answer.

"Latifah, Nasheeta, and Farrah," he said.

Zarifah clapped and laughed. "Very good."

"And what is your real name?" he asked. "Or is it a secret, for security reasons."

"Edith," she laughed. "Edith Smith. Which I'm hardly going to dance under. So I searched through a list of names, and picked the most unusual name I could find on the list, because it started with a 'Z', and now I am Zarifah!"

Everyone laughed, Cutter especially.

*She's charming. Entertaining, charming, and fascinating.*

"Since you brought up cultural appropriation, I will ask. Have you had any blowback, from your choice of names?"

"No, not really. There may be a rumbling here or there, but we're behaving in a way which is respectful of the cultures we are representing. We study the folkloric dances; the history, and we try to portray them in a good way. As long as we are showing honor toward them, most don't seen to mind. The custom of American's choosing Arabic dance names goes back to the 1980's, I believe, or maybe even further, and in Egypt dancers have stage names. So people are used to it."

"Besides, who doesn't love a belly dancer?" Saba said with a laugh. "Most people love us. Some love us a little bit too much."

Zarifah said, "Some of us need to keep our real names out of the public because of jobs, or family. And as you mentioned, there is a safety issue."

"I hope you are always safe," he said.

Watching him over her margarita glass, she sipped. "So, Cutter, what do you do?"

"I'm a Navy SEAL," he said.

"Really," her eyes widened, and she sat her glass down.

"Yes. Really." Ready to change the subject, he said, "Is dance your day job, or do you have another?"

"I teach gymnastics to children," she said.

"And I imagine you're quite good at that, after what I saw of your dancing tonight."

"A bit." She smiled.

"A bit?" Latifah laughed. "Don't let this girl fool you. She's an Olympic athlete."

"Excellent," he said. "Talented, and modest."

"Well, I didn't actually go to the Olympics, I was just in training for it."

"Why didn't you go?"

"Coaches told me I was too tall, and quit training me."

He frowned. "They don't sound like very good coaches."

"They were, and yet they weren't." She shrugged. "So now, I teach, and I dance for fun."

"Sounds like a good life," he said.

"It is," she agreed.

"Hey Amina, if we'd known a SEAL was in the audience, you wouldn't have had to have hired that bodyguard to protect Zarifa," Nasheeta said.

Cutter zeroed right in on Zarifah's face, which had paled, if it could pale, beneath all that makeup. Now he'd find out about those bruises.

"Why do you need a bodyguard?" He kept his facial expression and his voice calm, so as not to alarm her, but his alpha protective mode had kicked in. If there was a threat, he was ready.

"Because my ex fiancé decided to take a few swings at me," she said.

"A few swings," he said.

"But the police put him in jail, and now I have a restraining order against him," she added.

"That's like expecting a lock to keep a thief out." He shook his head. "Locks are for honest people. A determined thief will cut right through. It won't stop him. And a piece of paper won't stop a determined man."

"Well, it's all I have," she said.

"You don't carry?"

"A gun? I don't even know how to shoot." She gave a small shiver.

*Obviously, a woman who is afraid of guns. And me going out of town. Great.*

"But I bought some pepper spray," she smiled, and reached into her purse, pulling out her key ring from which dangled a pink plastic tube of pepper spray. She looked adorable with her little pink tube, and her hopeful sweet face, and he'd bet money she didn't know how to use it.

"Good," he said. "You keep that with you at all times, and practice with it."

"Practice?" She wrinkled up her forehead.

"Have you tried to use it?"

She shook her head no.

"When we get outside, I'll show you," he said.

The food came, and everyone dug in.

Too soon, dinner was over and it was time to go.

"I have to go out of town next week, but I'd like to call you, and make plans to get together, when I get home," Cutter said.

"Okay," Zarifah said. She held out her hand. "Give me your phone."

He handed it to her, and she put her number in.

"Thanks," he said.

"You're not going into danger, I hope," she said.

"Not next week," he said. "I've got to go visit my grand-mother. She's eighty."

"Aw, that's sweet," she said.

"But danger goes with my job," he said.

She blinked, taking that in.

*Might as well be totally honest with her from the start. No sugar coating anything. Only way to start a good relationship.*

"So this ex fiancé," he said. "Do you have a picture of him?"

"Why?"

"So I know what he looks like. To protect you."

"Oh."

"That's what I do, sweetheart. Protect. Serve. Defend."

She reached for her phone, scrolled through it, and found the pic. Thrusting it away from her, as if she couldn't stand to look at it, she pointed it at him. "That's him."

He looked at the pic. An Arab most likely from the look of him. Likely a wealthy one. He'd met many of that type.

"Got it." He nodded. "Thank you."

"Oh! No, thank you." She said. "For caring enough to want to protect me."

"Always," he said.

They gazed into each other eyes, the attraction strong.

He saw hope, trust, and wariness, as well as attraction in her eyes.

She didn't know him well enough yet. And that was all right. This was a good start.

"Thanks for your number," he said.

"You're welcome," she said. "Safe travels, and enjoy your grandma."

"Thank you. I intend to," he said. "Stay safe, Edith Smith."

Surprised, she realized she'd wanted to thank him for the flowers. He'd distracted her from that. "Thank you, for the flowers," she said.

"You're welcome. Thank you for your dance," he said, "and for inviting me to dinner with your friends."

Everyone stood to leave, and it got noisy as they all said their good nights.

When they came out of the restaurant, Cutter noted the black Mercedes again. This time, there were two men in the car, and they were watching the building. Cutter's senses went on immediate high alert.

There was no reason for the men to be sitting there watching them, unless their goal was to watch.

*Someone is being followed. Neither of the two men fit the picture she'd just showed me.*

He wondered who the men were, and who was being followed.

"Come over here," he said to Zarifah, and she moved toward him. He stood feeling the wind, so he could point her in the right direction, to spray her pepper spray.

She had it in her hand as if she didn't know how to hold it.

He showed her how to hold it, and how to spray it, and then said, "You'll want to note the wind, so that it doesn't blow back into your face."

"How can I do that if he's coming at me?" Her voice rose a bit with a degree of panic.

"You note it the minute you walk outside, then you're ready. Not the minute you see a guy coming at you. You're watching, being ready."

"Okay."

"Now try it."

After a couple sprays, he was satisfied that she at least knew how to shoot the spray.

He walked her to her car, and they said goodbye again.

Then he went to his car, got in and waited, until all the others had pulled away, and he continued watching, to see if the Mercedes would follow any of the ladies.

But none were followed.

Now the men were watching him.

He pulled out of the parking lot, and headed toward his home. Though he watched in his mirrors, the Mercedes didn't follow.

Though the men had done nothing to follow, he couldn't shake the feeling that something was off about those men, and that they were watching one of their party.

His intuition about such things had never been wrong.

# Chapter Six

Now that the Arabian Nights show was over, which was their big show of the year, the dancers could turn their full attentions to the new Shimmy Mob event. Amina had asked everyone to come to the studio five minutes early, before rehearsal if they could, so she could talk to them about Shimmy Mob.

"Team leaders have the music, and you'll get that from me. You'll need the edited version, which goes with the choreography, so don't go out and buy the other one. The correct one is five minutes long. I already have the edited version on my phone, if you'd like to listen to it now."

"Yes, I would," Zarifah said.

"Yes we want to hear it!" Latifah and Nasheeta chimed in together.

Amina found the song. "This is Shisha by Naked Rhythm." She hit play.

The music started and they all quietly listened to it.

"Oh I love it! So peppy," Bayda said.

"Yes, me too," Farrah said.

"Where are we going to dance?" Isis asked.

"I don't know yet," Amina said. "We have to line up a place. I sent a few messages already, to get things started. One to the mall, which should have a lot of foot traffic. We need a place we can dance free, since we're not selling tickets to offset that cost, and because this is a fundraiser."

"The mall would be great!" Bayda said.

"Lot's of shoppers and people to see us there," Saba said.

"I'm not sure how to collect money either, beyond passing baskets around, after we dance." Amina said. "I've never put together a fund raiser of any kind."

"What about an online site?" Isis asked. "One of the fundraiser ones?"

"Or you could use your dance site for the studio where students sign up for classes," Latifah said. "Since that's already set up to take payments."

"No, I don't want to co-mingle the money," Amina said. "That doesn't help; it just creates something to detangle later. This has to be totally separate from my business. I don't want anyone thinking everything isn't transparent, and above board, with the money."

"Yes, that makes sense," Latifah said.

"But an online donation site sounds good," Amina said. "And we'll need PR. I'm hoping for coverage, so we can get the word out."

* * *

The next day, Amirah and Zarifah met for tea ,and planning for Shimmy Mob, at a coffee shop not far from where Zarifah worked. After quick hugs, they went straight to business.

"Today was the last date for dancers to sign up," Amina said.

"How many do we have?" Zarifah asked.

"Thirty five! Isn't that wonderful?"

"Yes it is! Wow, so many! I don't think I even know that many dancers in town."

"We don't have all the dancers in town signed up, but we do have a good number of them," Amina said. "Most are from Riverton, some are from cities right next to us, but we also have two dancers coming from three hours away!"

Zarifah's eyes widened. "That's quite a drive just to dance."

"They believe in the cause, and we're the closest Shimmy Mob city to them."

"I still think that is quite admirable. They're going to have to drive the three hours, dance, and then drive three hours to get home, so that's six hours in a car. I know troupe dancers who won't go that far, even to dance at a paid gig."

"Yes, I know." Amina nodded.

They shared a glance, as they both knew the two dancers being referred to. But neither of them was going to gossip about them.

"I love this whole Shimmy Mob," Zarifah said. "I get excited every time I think about it."

"It's going to be amazing," Amina said.

"Have we got a site to dance at yet?"

"No" Amina shook her head. "That's proving to be a lot harder than I thought it would."

"Do you want me to help with that?"

"Yes, I would love your help," Amina said.

"Okay, I'll need a list of places you've tried already, so I don't repeat what you've done."

Amina opened her spiral notebook, and opened it to her list of possible sites.

Zarifah took out her phone, and took a picture of that page.

"Oh what a good idea," Amina said. "That saves time spent rewriting everything."

"Thanks, but it's not my original idea. Hassan used to take photos of my planner all the time." She tapped on the blue planner in her purse. "He said it was to keep track of when I was free to see him."

"If that was the case, then why did he always call you, when he knew we were together, and you were busy?"

"I don't know. I used to wonder the same thing. Now, I believe he was checking up on me, to see if I was where I'd said I would be. I took the app off my phone, after he went to jail."

"What app?"

"There's an app parents can use to track their children by cell phone, to make sure they're safe. He put it on my phone, supposedly for the same reason."

"That is so not okay for a boyfriend to do," Amira said. "Even if he is your fiancé."

"I know that now," Zarifah said. "But at the time, I just thought he was being protective, and wanted me to be safe."

"Wow. Well, I don't see how that would keep you safe," Amina said. "All it would do is tell him where you are, not fend off an attacker for you!"

"Right." Zarifa nodded. "He was very controlling. I see that now. Back then, I just thought he was being concerned, and protective."

"I'm so glad you're away from him." Amina reached out for her hand, and gave it a squeeze, and then she let loose, and her face lit up with happiness. "I did connect with the shelter, and have that part set up. They're thrilled we are doing this. I've got an appointment tomorrow with the director, and will get to tour the safe house during the day, when the children are at school, and the mom's are at job training, or counseling."

"Oh, that's wonderful," Zarifah said.

"If you'd like to go with me, as my assistant, that could be approved. But you have to promise never to reveal the location, not to write it down anywhere, or share it online. The location is a secret, and they're very careful who they tell about it."

"Wow. Yes, I'd love to take the tour," Zarifa said. "You know I'm discreet."

"Yes, I know you are, or I wouldn't have asked you." Amina nodded. "Okay, so I'll pick you up at eleven, and then we'll head there. Then lunch afterward, if you have the time."

"I have the time," Zarifah said.

Cutter texted Zarifah

*How's rehearsal going? Have you practiced with your pepper spray?*

She answered him.

*Rehearsal hasn't started yet. And we haven't found a place to dance. Thanks for the reminder about the pepper spray. Got to dance now.*

She put her phone away, and prepared to dance as the other dancers entered the studio's.

"Bad news. The mall is out," Amina said. "They want us to carry a million dollars worth of insurance, just to dance there for less than ten minutes."

"That's crazy," Latifah said.

"Whatever it is, I don't have that kind of money," Amina said.

"Oh no. So, we can't dance at the mall," Bayda said.

"What are our other options?" Saba asked. "Are there other places you've checked out?"

"But all we're trying to do is raise funds for the domestic abuse shelter," Nasheeta said. "Don't they understand that?"

"They do," Amina said. "But one of the problems is, it's a flash mob, and some flash mobs around the county have been destructive and disruptive. So their insurance company won't cover events like ours, in case something goes wrong. That throws everything on us."

They were back to the drawing board and still had to find a site.

* * *

The next day, Amina picked Zarifah up, and drove to the shelter.

The shelter didn't have a mailbox with numbers, or any numbers marking the house from the street. An older two-story building, it had an enclosed front porch, with high brick walls, over six foot tall, and screens across the top, between the porch walls, and the roof.

"Wow, they've done a good job hiding them away," Zarifah said.

"Yes, they have. I'm impressed," Amina said. She drove her small silver Honda up the drive, and stopped in front of a gated back yard. More brick walls, and a strong electric gate.

Rolling down her window, she went to press a button, but a voice came through the speakers beating her to it.

"Ms. Crandall?"

"Yes. I'm here with Edith Smith. We have an appointment with Margot Chadron, the director of your center."

"We're expecting you. Please park in the first spot by the back door." The gate door started to slowly swing open.

"Thank you."

Amina rolled her window back up, and drove through the gate that began to close behind her, once the car was through.

"It feels like they're watching us," Zarifah said.

"Because they are," Amina said. "They have to watch."

"I understand, I'm just not used to this."

"Me either, but I understand the need for it. That makes it easier. And knowing it keeps the women and children safe, and the women who work here, I feel safer, actually. No one's crazy ex is going to be able to come in here, and hurt people."

"That is a very good thing." Zarifah nodded her head emphatically.

Amina had parked, while they were talking, and now she turned off the car, and they got out to walk toward the back door.

The door opened, and a short black woman stood holding the door and smiling. "Welcome," she said. "We're all so excited for what you are doing for the shelter. Come on in."

They went up the concrete steps and followed her inside.

Saturday was the night before the big day. It was their final rehearsal, and everyone was excited to see what color the Shimmy Mob t-shirts were.

Amina, as the team leader knew, because the box was shipped to her, but she'd kept the secret, even from Zarifah.

"What can it be?" Bayda asked. "I can't wait to see them."

"You haven't even opened the box yet?" Zarifah was amazed.

"Oh, I peeked just a little," Amina, said, "I know what color they are, but I closed the box back up again."

Zarifah laughed.

"Sneaky," Bayda said. "I'd have peeked too."

"Help me hand them out?" Amina asked Zarifah.

"Yes, of course," Zarifah said.

Amina sat the box on the floor, pulled the tape off the top, and then reached her hand inside, her eyes twinkling, and her mouth turning up in a smile, as she teased. "Everyone ready?" she asked.

"Yes," the chorus of women replied.

She whisked out a red t-shirt, and held it up. "It's red!"

"Oh good," Zarifah said. "I love it!"

"Of course you do. Red is your color." Amina laughed.

The women had swarmed around them, to get their shirts, and as Amina read off each name and corresponding size, each dancer got her t-shirt.

Some of the dancers tried their t-shirts on right away, and some knew their-shirt would fit, so they tucked their shirts into their dance bags.

Latifah, stuck trying to put on a shirt, which was too small for her, ended up trading with Nasheeta, whose shirt was too big. Finally, each dancer had a shirt, which fit well enough, and they were happy.

"Okay ladies," Amina clapped her hands to get their attention again. "Ladies! Time to rehearse!"

Everyone lined up and she started the music.

* * *

With every Saturday scheduled as a Shimmy Mob rehearsal day, and two nights each week, Zarifah had less time for dating, than she ordinarily had. In between learning the dance, she was also trying to help Amina find a site for them to dance at.

Cutter was understanding and patient. Qualities she'd put on her wish list for the perfect man for her.

This time she was going to be picky, because she'd been far too understanding, and forgiving before.

This time she wanted what she wanted.

And if she couldn't have the kind of man she wanted, she was far too busy anyway.

But even with everything going on, Zarifah and Cutter kept bumping into each other, as if fate was knocking them together, to make sure they connected.

The first time it happened, she'd just finished teaching one of her classes, and was coming out of her rental space, and heading to the Deli, a couple of stores down, when she saw him coming out of the barber shop, with a shorter, new haircut.

"Cutter, what are you doing here?" she asked.

He pointed to his head and grinned, then said, "I might ask you the same."

"I just finished teaching a class, and am on my dinner break," she said. "I'm heading to the Deli, would you like to join me?"

"I would," he said, with a grin. "Perfect timing."

"It is," she agreed. The butterflies in her stomach were now doing summersaults, and she was hungry. It was so nice to have company, and not be eating alone, and especially nice to be eating with him.

"So you teach here?" he asked. "I didn't know that. But I come here all the time to get my hair cut. I wonder why we've never bumped into each other before?"

"I don't know," she said. "It wasn't the right timing I guess."

"Timing is everything," he said. "Fate turns on a dime."

"True," she said. "I guess we just got lucky." She watched him open the door for her, and then she walked into the deli.

*How did I get so lucky? What are the odds of me bumping into him like this?*

The second time it happened, she was at the library returning books, when she heard a voice behind her, that gave her butterflies in her stomach.

"I'd say we have to stop meeting like this," he said.

She whirled around to see him, with a big smile. "Cutter!"

He continued. "But that's such a cliché, and whatever is making this happen, I hope it keeps up."

"It is kind of fun, isn't it?"

"Have time to go for a coffee?"

"I do. Your timing is good," she nodded.

"It's not me arranging it," he said. "But I'll happily take it."

The third time, she was pumping gas, when he pulled up at the pump next to her, got out, came around, and said, "Here, let me help you with that."

He was such a gentleman, and these little surprises were so nice, and becoming so frequent, that she found herself fussing with her hair and makeup, before she left her apartment to go anywhere.

Had he not been so surprised himself at these happenings, and they not been so random, she'd have thought he was following her, and setting the meetings up. But each time had felt so genuine, and the surprise and pleasure she saw in his face, made her think this was real. She didn't think he could've been faking it, or setting it up.

Besides, he was sometimes brutally honest. That had taken a little getting used to, but after the smooth moves of Hassan, she found that she actually liked his way much better.

*Honesty was a solid foundation for any kind of relationship.*

She would even bet that, if she asked him if a dress made her fat and it did, he'd tell her yes. It wasn't a bad thing to have someone in your life like that.

After the third time they bumped into each other, on the following day, she started looking for him everywhere she went. But she didn't bump into him then.

Maybe she was trying too hard.

Her phone did ring that night, however, and it was Cutter.

"Hello," she said.

"Let's put our schedules together, and schedule a real date," he said. "I want to take you to dinner somewhere nice, so you can relax."

"Oh that sounds nice," she said. "I'd like that."

"Have your planner handy?"

"Yes. It's right here in my purse."

They settled on a date, and she wrote it in her planner.

"Can we go somewhere that has steaks?" she asked. "I've been hungry for a big steak."

"I bet you're not getting enough protein. When was the last time you had steak?"

"I can't even remember," she said.

"Then a steakhouse it is. I know a good one. Pick you up at six."

"That's perfect."

When the day came of their first official date, she thought back over their get togethers, which had come before. It really didn't feel like a first date, as they'd been getting together a little bit here, and a little bit there.

He texted her every couple of days to see how she was doing. Partly he was making sure she was safe, which she appreciated.

*He really is such a thoughtful man. It's good to know he cares.*

She stared into her closet, wondering what to wear. Not one of her tight, skinny dresses, because she really was hungry. But not something loose and baggy, either.

Was there nothing in between?

She sighed and reached for the snug, royal blue dress, which everyone said brought out the blue in her eyes. Likely she'd have to get a doggie bag for half her steak.

By six she was ready, and Cutter was prompt on the dot. Her doorbell rang ,and she hurried to open it, stepping into her shoes just before.

When she open the door, his eyes widened in appreciation. He whistled a low, slow whistle, and she watched his lips.

She smiled up at him. "Hello," she said. "You look wonderful too."

He really did, in a dark suit, white shirt, and dark red tie. He could've stepped out of a movie, or a fashion catalog, he looked so good.

"Come on in," she said.

"It's a bit chilly. You may need a sweater, or wrap, but it's a shame having to cover you up, in that dress," he said.

"I'll just get my wrap," she said, and went back into the bedroom.

He watched her walk away, and he watched her walk back, pulling the wrap around her shoulders. He watched as if he'd like to unwrap her.

Holding her elbow, he escorted her to the car, and opened the door. He waited while she climbed in.

A single red rose sat on the dash, right in front of her.

"You like to spoil me with flowers," she said.

"Yes," he said. "That I do." Then he closed the door, and walked around to his side.

Once in the car, he turned soft violin music on, and then pulled out of the parking lot.

He was a romantic sort of man.

She glanced at him, and wondered how he would be in bed. If he would make love slow. She hoped he would.

# Chapter Seven

She watched his hands as he drove.

After a while, he said, "You're very quiet."

"I'm just enjoying the music, and the ride," she said. "You were right. I do need a nice dinner, and to relax. I've been going nonstop."

"We're going to a small restaurant, where you should be able to do just that. It's less than an hour away, and worth the drive," he said. "They've converted a house into a restaurant, and the separate rooms created a small, cozier feeling, than most steakhouses."

"Oh that sounds nice," she said.

"I didn't see what was in your stack of books the other day," he said. "But it was quite a tall stack. What do you like to read?"

"Oh, a little bit of everything," she said. "Mystery, romance, romantic suspense, history. What do you like to read?"

"Fiction with action in it, history, nonfiction, military, biographies. Lots of things."

"Wow, you read a lot too."

"When I have time."

"It's probably hard to do, when they deploy you all over the world."

"I read when and where I can. It's relaxing for me. But if I get too caught up in a book, that could be a bad thing. So no, not so much during deployments. I'll tear through a stack, when I'm in the states though."

An image of the two of them, curled up on a couch or in bed, each with their books, reading, entered her mind.

One of the things on her list of qualities for a good boyfriend was, loves to read.

They reached the restaurant, and he pulled the car into the parking lot and parked. "This is it," he said.

She put her hand on the door handle.

"Stay put." He opened his door, got out, and came around to open her door.

It was so nice, the way he treated her like a lady, opening doors. He was always a gentleman, and tonight he looked so handsome.

Inside the steakhouse were small rooms, each with several tables covered with white tablecloths, and small vases of flowers with lit candles in the middle.

An intimate, romantic place was where he'd taken her on their first "official" date, and it was lovely.

After they were seated, and the waiter had poured water for them, and handed them their menus, she asked, "Do you have any suggestions? What is good?"

"Everything is good, madam," he said.

"Order anything you want," Cutter said. "If that's the Porterhouse, then get that."

"That is for two, sir," their waiter said.

"Yes," Cutter replied. "I know."

"That's two steaks," she said. "I can't eat two steaks."

"You said you were powerfully hungry for steak," Cutter teased her. "I'm just letting you know to order as much as you want."

"I could never eat a New York strip and a tenderloin, even at my hungriest," she said with a laugh "But it says here, that it's for two, and we could share one. I've never done that before."

"Never? Well then, you're in for a treat. That's what we'll do."

"Porterhouse for two is a twenty two ounce, thick cut, served with roasted red potatoes, sautéed wild onions, vegetable of the day, and house rosemary demi glace. You may substitute a salad for the vegetable, or order a salad on the side," the waiter paused, waiting for them to speak.

"What is the vegetable?" she asked.

"Today vegetable is, roasted Brussels sprouts."

"Oh, I'm not a fan of Brussels sprouts," she said.

"You wish the salad instead?"

"Yes. Salad for me," she said. "Ranch dressing if you have it."

"We do." The waiter nodded. "And for you sir?"

"I'll have a salad as well," Cutter said. "Thousand Island."

"Very good sir." He left to put their order in.

"We can share part of each steak, and that way you'll have tried everything."

"Sounds good to me," she said.

The waiter returned with hot fresh bread and butter.

"Oh, this is one of my weaknesses," she said. "Fresh bread."

Cutter took the serrated knife, and cut slices of the bread for them. "Then enjoy," he said. "Tonight is all about treating you."

"It is?" That surprised her.

Usually, dates were about a man trying to impress her.

Watching Cutter, she realized he behaved as if he had no need to impress anyone.

*I guess being a SEAL is impressive enough. They know what they can do, and don't have to prove anything to anybody.*

He was the most truly confident male she'd ever met. It was a quiet confidence.

"So, if you hadn't gone into the SEAL's, or the Navy, what would you have done?" she asked, taking a piece of bread, and reaching for the butter.

He handed the small butter plate to her. "I might've ended up working in my grandfather's nursery, raising flowers," he said.

"That's why you know what you do about flowers."

"Yes." He nodded. "But as much as I enjoyed helping grandfather, I wanted to be a SEAL more than anything else. I thought about it night and day. Was obsessive about it, I wanted it so bad."

"Wow. Was your grandfather disappointed?"

"If he was, he never said. He did say that he was proud."

"Well I should think so," she said.

*I don't dare ever tell him, that when I first met him, I thought he might be gay. I must've been out of my mind. He's the manliest man I've ever met. He just happens to like flowers and dancers.*

"Penny for your thoughts," he said.

"Oh no," she said. "I can't."

"Now I'm even more intrigued."

"No, really, I can't," she laughed. "And anyway, it's ridiculous."

"And still you won't share it with me? Is it that bad?"

"I don't want to ruin our date."

"Nothing you say could ruin our date."

She raised an eyebrow.

"Okay now we are veering in a direction which concerns me. Instead of the two of us having fun, there's a weird vibe moving in, which needs sorted out."

"If I tell you, you have to promise you won't get mad."

"I doubt anything you say would make me mad."

She raised her eyebrow again.

"Look, I'm not going to get angry at anything you say."

"Okay." She took a deep breath. "I thought, when we first met, you know, at the theater, and you liked dance and flowers..."

He started laughing, and said, "You thought I was gay."

She shrugged. "Well, flowers and dance."

He shook his head. "That's ridiculous. Before I met you, I dated lots of women. Mostly strippers."

"Oh."

"Yes, oh."

"What made you stop? Dating strippers."

"They never wanted to kiss."

"I like kissing." She smiled at him; glad he wasn't angry with her.

"I like long kissing sessions, the kind that steam the car up."

"Oh yes, I like those too."

The rest of their dinner went well, and soon they were back at her apartment.

He walked her to the door, and waited while he fished his keys out.

"Would you like to come in?" she asked. "And, stay for coffee?"

"I'd much rather stay for kisses," he said. "If you're offering kisses."

She turned to face him. "Oh yes," she said. "I'm definitely offering those."

*Always ask for what you want,* he thought. *That almost always pays off.*

He'd missed kisses, and long make out sessions, with a woman he cared about.

Since he'd met Zarifah, kissing her had been foremost on his mind.

*Much can depend on a first kiss. It sets the tone for the relationship. And this first kiss has waited long enough.*

Cutter bent to kiss her, not waiting for her to finish unlocking the door. His lips descended to meet hers, lightly brushing them at first, then he kissed her softly.

Her lips parted as she kissed him back, her arms reaching up around his neck.

He slid his hands around her waist, to her back, and pulled her closer. His tongue teased her lips, light and playful.

She opened her lips wider, her tongue coming to meet his, the tip teasing him back.

Their tongues met, touched, teased, danced.

He grew hungry for her, and she for him, and the kiss deepened, her breath coming shorter, her hands holding on tight.

Instead of breaking the kiss, he moved her back against the door, and finding the key in it, turned and opened the door, while still kissing her.

Cutter moved her into the apartment, closed the door behind them, and flipped the lock. Then he placed both hands on her hips, and guided her, as he kissed her, through the front room, into the bedroom behind it.

Still kissing her, he backed her up to the bed, until the backs of her knees met the bed.

When she felt the bed behind her knees, she gave way, sinking down onto the bed, and pulling Cutter down with her as they continued to kiss.

His hands left her hips, and moved slowly up her sides, where he found a zipper on one side of her dress. She was now flat on the bed.

He raised his head, letting them both come up for air.

"Still too many clothes," she said.

"I agree," he said. "Let's lose them."

"My dress is not easy to get into, or out of," she said.

"I can help you with that," he said.

He unzipped her dress, kissed her neck, and then turned her around to kiss her lips.

Their first kiss had gone so well, he couldn't wait to see how their first long make out session would be. He intended to take things slow with her, and do no more than to kiss her as much as she wanted, and anywhere she wanted.

Kissing her was something he could do all day.

* * *

International Belly Dance Day was here, and the first Shimmy Mob flash mob event was happening. It was May first, 2011, and they would be making history.

Zarifah could hardly wait. She'd dressed an hour before she'd had to, and was dancing in her apartment, not caring if she bumped into anything, or knocked anything over.

She'd made her place danceable again, and reveled in that freedom.

While it might not be decorated as prettily, or as richly as it had been before, the space was hers, she was free, and she was dancing.

Turning on the music again, she danced, and laughed.

The joy was back in her soul, and dancing Shimmy Mob had given it back to her.

When the knock came on the door, it surprised her. She turned off the music, and went to the door and peeked out.

*Cutter.*

He stood holding one single red rose. Dressed all in black, he was the most handsome man she'd ever seen.

She felt like the luckiest woman in the world.

Though she'd been full of joy before, her heart now soared with happiness, as she opened the door.

"Hello," she said. "Just when I thought this day couldn't get any better."

"Brought you something," he said, handing her the rose.

"You spoil me," she said, her smile from ear to ear.

"You're worth spoiling," he said, giving her a warm smile.

She let him in, and went to put the rose in a vase with water.

* * *

Her happy face and sparking eyes greeted Cutter, when she opened the door.

Seeing her happy sent a smile across his face.

She took his breath away.

When she went to put the flower in her vase, he watched her move, her gracefulness, and strength. The careful way she put the flower in water, and set it on the table, that happy smile on her face.

He wanted to kiss her, but waited.

As if she'd read his mind, she set the flower on the table, and then came to him, putting her palms on his chest, looking up into his eyes, stretching up for a kiss.

Their lips met, and time slipped by, as they tasted and touched each other.

A beep made them break apart. It was followed by another beep.

His watch and her phone had gone off at the same time.

"Didn't want you to be late," he said.

"I set an alarm too," she said. "Oh, we need to go."

"There's time," he said. He knew there was no rush and she was just excited. They had plenty of time to get to the farmers market where the women would dance. "Are you ready?"

* * *

Next to the Riverton farmer's market, was an empty area, between a parking lot full of cars, and the fruit and vegetable stalls, where the local Shimmy Mob dancers would perform.

Cutter watched Zarifa, as she greeted the other dancers and they looked around the area they would be dancing. He loved seeing how excited she was, and how happy.

The excitement he'd seen building in her, the way she'd blossomed in the few weeks he'd known her, was a thing of beauty.

Zarifah had gone from being a victim, to being a survivor, to being a thriver.

He was so damn proud of her.

The dance group needed pictures and video of their dance, to be shared on social media, one of the things Shimmy Mob International had asked each team to send in, so each dancer had asked her family and friends to come out to watch them perform, and to take pictures and video.

Several of them had shown up, but there'd been no discussion of who was doing what, so Cutter opted for video. He had a good camera on his phone, and his hand was steady.

There would be at least one video they could count on.

Taking his cell phone, Cutter found a spot on the left side of the performance area, which was perfect for taking photos or video, and waited for them to go on.

He spotted Zarifah in the crowd, waited for her to see him, and then nodded to her.

She smiled, and waved back, clearly exited, as joy shone in her face and movements.

He returned a smile, happy to see her enjoying herself. Then he turned his head to scan the area, taking in the venders, the shoppers and browsers, and the occasional man standing by himself, likely waiting on his woman, as Cutter was. The farmer's market was busier than he'd expected, but then he didn't shop at farmer's markets. Instead, he went to the grocery.

Other than a few curious glances at the dancers, who were gathering together, wearing red Shimmy Mob t-shirts, which were eye catching red with white lettering, most shoppers were busy shopping.

It was a peaceful crowd.

Cutter's habit of scanning a crowd was momentarily interrupted, when Zarifah and the other dancers, moved into the open area, to begin their five-minute dance.

Amina, the Shimmy Mob team leader, spoke into a

microphone, getting everyone's attention, and explained why they were there to dance, what Shimmy Mob was, and the local shelter they were raising funds for.

Cutter listened to her as he scanned the crowd again.

People were moving near to the dance area, and had turned their attention to the dancers.

Done speaking, the director signaled someone, who turned the music on.

The dancers moved out into the center of the pavement, then turned as one, and went into the number.

Holding his cell phone steady, to video their dance, as he'd promised her, Cutter watched with his own eyes to see her fully, and to make eye contact if she looked his way.

He could've watched Zarifah for hours, the way she moved, her long arms and legs graceful, yet strong.

The smile she wore on her face today spoke of triumph and happiness. She had a glow.

Her eyes met his, and the heat between them sizzled.

He sent her a smile.

Her smile deepened, the joy spreading.

She was the most beautiful dancer he'd ever seen, dancing in her joy.

He watched her throughout the entire dance, and as she took her final pose, with all the other dancers, he ended the video, before he slipped his phone into his pocket.

*Crack.*

Horror filled her eyes, erasing everything good, as the loud crack of a bullet broke through the noise of many hands clapping.

Cutter jerked his head around, and his sharp gaze went toward the area where the gunman must be, his hand automatically reaching for his side arm, as women and children screamed and ran in all directions.

Pulling out his side arm, the gun was in his hand, a movement as natural to him as breathing, as all his training kicked in.

*Where's the gunman?*

# Chapter Eight

Cutter searched for his mark, as men, women and children ran, right and left, screaming. Innocents.

The gunman wouldn't be running. He'd fired at the dancers, but none had fallen. With nothing but cars in the lot behind the dancers, he had to be shooting at the dancers.

*Who is his target?*

Cutter's gaze searched and locked, onto an olive skinned man, with a beard, who hadn't been there before.

The man turned his head, giving Cutter a glimpse.

*Hassan.*

His angry gaze was searching for Zarifah, who Cutter could still see in his peripheral vision, as he kept one eye on her, while he prepared to get his mark in the cross hairs. Protecting his woman, who'd shuffled in one direction, and then another, more to dodge dancers who were running past her, than out of any instinct to move, before freezing, with her eyes as wide as a deer frozen in bright headlights.

Neither flight nor fight, she froze.

Rage filled Cutter. But then he focused, still as a rock, as his vision kept an eye on her, while getting his mark in the cross hairs as his training kicked in.

Zero in on target. Mark. Aim. Shoot.

*Crack.*

Clear shot. Repeat. Mark. Aim. Shoot.

*Crack.*

The fast sequence of a double tap. *Over and done.*

Hassan's head jerked back, both shots true to target, and then he went down, his gun arm dropping down toward the ground, the gun no longer aiming toward anyone.

The echo of Cutters firearm had caused even more hysteria among the general population, as more women's high-pitched screams filled the air.

"Everyone stay calm!" he yelled.

With a quick glance to Zarifah, he saw she stood frozen, still.

The only one still in the dance area. She appeared not to have been hit, just scared.

He scanned the area again, looking for a second man.

Seeing no other threat to her, Cutter burst into a run.

He ran over to where the man fell; ready to shoot again, if needed.

Reaching Hassan, he kicked away the man's gun, to where Hassan couldn't reach it. Then he knelt, checking for other weapons, and checking to be sure the man was dead.

Confirmed. Dead.

*Zarifah.*

He looked back to where she'd been standing.

*She's gone.*

He stood, his eyes searching for her. From the last look he'd seen in her eyes, she'd been terrified. He needed to find her. Calm her. Let her know it was over, and she was safe now.

But he didn't see her.

*Has she been hit?*

He could've sworn she hadn't been. He ran toward the space where she'd been standing, and his eyes searched for where she might've gone. Then he heard her.

Weeping. *Not far.*

She was behind the closest stall to where they'd been dancing.

He placed his gun in its holster, and moved her way. Moving into the stall, he saw her, curled up beneath the wooden stand, her knees folded in, her arms wrapped over her bent head, covering her ears, as she shook and cried.

"Don't kill me, please," she begged. "I'll go with you, I promise."

It hit him in the gut, seeing her like this and hearing her beg.

"Zarifah," he called her name. "It's Cutter." He squatted down next to her. "You're safe. He's dead."

Still shaking, she peered between her arms, but kept her arms still wrapped around her head.

She saw him, and then she whispered, "He's dead?"

"Yes, he's dead. He won't ever hurt you again."

Her arms fell slowly away from her head, as if completely exhausted, and tears came rushing out now, as she released what her fear had held back.

Knowing she needed to be grounded, to touch something solid, he took hold of her arm and pulled her nearer, as he sat on the ground, then wrapping his arms around her, he held her close.

She clutched onto him, still shaking and crying.

He kissed the top of her head as he continued to hold her. "I've got you, babe. You're all right. I've got you."

Her sobs turned to hiccups, which shook her diaphragm.

She leaned into him, seeking his warmth and strength, moving slightly, as if she'd burrow into his skin, as if she couldn't get close enough.

His arms tightened around her, tight as he could make them, without hurting her, letting her know, by the fierceness of the hug that she was safe and protected. Cared for.

Her hiccups slowed, and then stopped.

Taking one hand, he stroked her head, her silky hair, treating her with the tenderness she deserved.

He wanted to take away her fear, her pain, her bad memories, and was waiting for her to calm, and know it was over, and she was all right. He repeated the words. "You're all right, babe. It's over."

Taking a deep, jerking breath, she leaned her head back, to look up at him. "It really is over? He's gone?"

"Yes," keeping his voice firm and strong, to reinforce that one word, he answered her.

She took another deep breath, the remaining tension making it jerky.

He cupped the sides of her face with both hands, and their eyes connected like an intense lock.

"Breathe," he said.

She took a breath, but not a deep enough one, like he'd wanted her to take.

"Deep breath," he said. "Again."

She sucked in a deep breath, and without breaking their gaze, breathed.

"Again," he said.

Following his commands, she slowly calmed her breath, her heart rate, and her mind, until she reached a state of calm.

He saw it in her, felt it in her, and heard it in her.

They'd never been as close as they were in this moment.

And then, he kissed her.

His lips descended, his hands still holding her face in his palms, his lips soft upon her lips, the most gentle of kisses, letting her know she was loved, treasured and cared for.

With a soft sigh, she responded, her lips parting, her breath slowly escaping, her lips and tongue ready to follow his lead.

His tongue had just met hers, when he heard sirens nearing.

*Police had arrived. Likely ambulance too.*

The sirens startled her again. Her startle reflex was ramped up from her experience.

He pressed his lips against hers, once more, and then, ending the kiss said, "We'd better stand now. The police will need to take our statements."

Dazed by the kissing, and the events, her eyes now widened. "Oh, police. Right. He's not allowed to come near me. I have the restraining order, in my purse."

"He can't come near anyone. He's dead," he reminded her, since she'd spoken as if Hassan were still alive.

It hadn't fully sunk in yet.

"But I'm glad you have the document with you," he said. "That will help, when you give your statement to the police."

"You, you shot him, didn't you?" She asked, her tone not sure.

*Good. She hadn't seen.*

He'd been hoping she hadn't.

*She'd had enough traumas, and didn't need to see that.*

"Yes," he said. "I shot him."

"I'm glad," she said. "I'm so glad."

"Come on," he helped her to stand.

Once she was up, he slid one arm around her waist, keeping her close.

She leaned in toward him, still drawing from his strength. "I'm so glad you were here," she said, "If you hadn't been..." Her eyes gazing up at him, widened, at the thought of what might've happened.

"I'm glad I was here too." He gave her a squeeze.

She was soaking up the physical attention like a thirsty sponge. But she was also a distraction.

Police were moving around the farmers market, assessing the situation.

His guns were holstered, but he would need to declare them, and give his statement. He needed to redirect her thoughts now. "Do you have your purse?"

"No. I hope it's where I put it before we danced."

"Show me where." He had a pretty good idea where it was, but this would redirect her thoughts, giving her something to do.

"Okay."

Sticking by her side, he let loose of her, and took her by the hand.

She walked toward the tree, where the dancers had put their things, with a companion there to watch them.

No one was there now, but her purse was still where she'd left it.

She picked it up, and then looked at him, unsure what to do next.

"Come on," he said. "They'll want to take our statements."

All the dancers were gathered in one area, far away from the spot where the body lay sprawled on the concrete.

Police had taped off the area where the body lay, and officers were taking down names, and asking questions.

"We might be here for a while," he said, "Go with your friends, and tell the police what you know. They'll want to talk to me separately. Don't worry if they separate us. You're safe now." He squeezed her hand, before letting go.

A policeman walked up to them, one hand on his gun. "Sir, do you have weapons to declare?"

He raised his hands away from his weapons. "Yes sir, I do. Two guns. One my side arm, and one on my calf."

The officer started to remove Cutter's weapons, patting him down, as another officer watched, ready with his gun.

Once they'd removed his forty caliber Sig Sauer side arm, and the thirty-eight revolver on his calf, along with a six-inch blade folding Buck knife, and with a three-inch bladed knife, Officer Kelly said, "Those are a lot of weapons for a civilian to carry. You active duty?"

"Yes, sir."

Officer Kelly nodded. "Figured as much. They're singing your praises, over there." He nodded toward the group of women in the red t-shirts. "Everybody loves a SEAL. One of them got the whole thing on video. It's clear you saved many lives today. I'm still going to need your ID, and your statement. Step over here with me, and we'll sit in the privacy of the squad car, away from your new fan club."

"Yes sir." All of this was expected. He had after all, just killed a man. Even if he'd saved lives by doing it.

An hour later, the homicide detective cleared Cutter to go. They gave him all his weapons back, except for the gun he'd used, telling him that he could have it back after the investigation was over.

Cutter now knew a lot more than he had previously about Zarifah's ex fiancé, Hassan.

Like the fact that he wasn't a U.S. citizen. Perhaps that was one reason he'd been upset about Zarifah cancelling their engagement. He'd have been able to stay in the country longer, if he'd married her.

And he was a person of interest, on one of the watch lists, with a watch only status. They didn't tell him why. He wasn't going to ask.

The man was no longer a threat to anyone.

Vendors had given their information to police, and then had closed up for the day.

No one was going to be selling anything, right next to the crime scene, and most likely everyone just wanted to go home to his, or her, comfortable familiar places where they'd feel safe.

Zarifah had been very shaken up by the events, and he needed to see her up close, and assess how she was dealing with it.

*Hopefully she'd been checked for shock.*

An EMT could treat her, there were plenty standing by.

She was sitting near a closed fruit stand, with one of her dance friends, waiting. Probably waiting on him. The other dancers had all gone home.

He was glad that at least one of them had stayed with her.

"Ready to go home?" he asked.

"I am," she said. "Cutter, this is my friend, Bayda."

"Pleased to meet you," he said.

The woman grasped his outstretched hand enthusiastically. "Thank you, for saving our lives," she said. "We owe so much to you."

"You don't owe me a thing," he said, as he finished shaking her hand, and then let go.

"I told everyone to go on home," Zarifah said. "Bayda wouldn't leave."

"You're not getting rid of me that easy," Bayda said. "And we weren't going to leave you here, by yourself. Especially after what almost happened. Belly dance sisters look out for each other. That's what sisters are supposed to do."

"Thanks for staying with Zarifah," Cutter said. "I'm glad she has a good friend like you."

Bayda beamed.

"I want to tell the officers something," Zarifah said.

"Sure honey," Cutter put his arm around her. "Come on. They won't mind."

She'd seemed hesitant about talking to them; he could hear it in her voice.

They walked over to the officers together.

"Excuse me," she said, not quite loud enough, and then she cleared her throat, and said it again. "Excuse me,"

The officers turned to look at her.

"It's why we were dancing today," she said. "Shimmy Mob raises funds for our local domestic abuse center."

"Never heard of it," officer Owens said.

"That's because it's brand new," she said. "This is our first year."

"Awesome," he said. "Next time though, you need to get a permit. Get permissions. We can't really condone mobs, even for a good reason."

As they turned to go, Officer Kelly came up to Zarifah. "Let us know when and where you're dancing, so we can come by, and keep an eye on the crowd. Keep you safe, while you're dancing." he winked at her.

"I've got my own SEAL right here," she said, looking up at Cutter. "He does a real good job protecting me."

"Yes, ma'am, he does," officer Kelly agreed. "More than you may know."

"Good night," she said with a smile, waving at the police officers.

Surprised, the officers waved back at her, smiling and said, "good night."

Zarifah and Bayda gave each other hugs, and then Cutter watched to be sure Bayda was safe in her car, before she drove away.

"You've had quite a day," he said to Zarifah, as he watched her friend, making sure she was safe.

"Quite a day, yes," she said. "I really just feel like curling up somewhere."

"Do you want to curl up at home, or do you want to curl up at my place, and watch a movie? Just snuggle. Til you fall asleep," he said.

"That sounds wonderful," she breathed the words out, as if each word was releasing stress she'd held.

"Good," he said, putting his arm around her, and guiding her toward his car. "So home, or my place?"

She obviously wanted to snuggle, as she'd made no choice.

"Your place," she said. "Snuggling sounds really good."

"I thought it might," he said.

"The police officer who took my statement, took my order of protection, wrote down some stuff about it, and then handed it backing saying 'These don't always work. Sometimes they make matters worse,'" she said.

"No piece of paper is going to stop a man intent on doing harm."

"I'm glad you stopped him," Zarifah said. "If not for you, I'd be dead right now."

"How about we celebrate that. I remember you don't

eat, before you dance, and you need to eat something. Want to order a pizza?" he asked. "Pizza and a movie, and snuggle?"

"That sounds really good," she smiled. "Especially the snuggle part. I don't care if we have pizza, or whatever you want. But can we have ice cream? I'm really wanting ice cream."

"Of course. What kind of ice cream do you want?"

*Ice cream must be her comfort food*, he thought. *I wonder what her favorite is?*

"Some kind with chocolate."

"We'll stop on the way to my place, and pick up whatever you want."

# Chapter Nine

Back at his apartment, she went into his bathroom to freshen up, while he put the ice cream and other purchases away.

She came back out. "I need a shower," she said. "I'm sticky and stinky."

"Go ahead." He said. "I'm going to order the pizza. What would you like on it?"

"It doesn't matter," she said.

"What kind do you like, when you're hungry for pizza?"

"Mushroom, onion, olives."

"We can do that," he said, picking up the phone. "Go ahead and hop in. I want one too."

In the bathroom she found a clean thick towel and a washcloth. Peeling off her clothes, she turned on the shower. Warm water streaming, she stepped in.

When she stepped out again, she saw he'd placed one of his clean t-shirts on top of the sink for her. She was glad of it, as she hadn't brought clean clothes with her. She dried off, and pulled the t-shirt on, feeling how soft it was. It had seen many washings, and she wondered if it was one of his favorites.

It felt nice wearing his shirt. The shirt came just to the bottom of her buttocks, so she pulled her panties back on. She did feel a whole lot better, and now she'd smell better too.

Rubbing her hair with the towel, she walked back out, carrying the rest of her dance clothes.

He stood in the kitchen, pulling out two paper plates and some napkins. There were two water bottles on the counter.

He pointed to them and said, "Hydrate."

She went over to her bag, tossed her clothes down next to it, and then came back for the water bottle.

"Do you like hard boiled eggs?" he asked.

"Yes, why?"

He opened the fridge, reached in, and then pulled out an egg and offered it to her. "Because you need protein, and our pizza doesn't meet that need. Here," he said. "There's salt on the table if you need it."

She took the egg from him, and sat at the kitchen table, tapping it to crack the shell off. "Do you eat like this all the time?" she asked.

"What, eat protein?" He looked at her. "Of course, don't you?"

"I tend to just not eat, to keep my weight down. I can't eat before I dance."

"So what have you eaten today?"

"Piece of toast and jelly."

He shook his head at her. "That's nothing."

"I eat a lot, after I dance, to make up for it."

"So you need that protein now." He sat the water bottle

on the table next to her, and then said, "I'm going to hop in the shower. Won't be long."

"Okay."

Five minutes later he was back, with a towel wrapped around his waist. He saw she'd eaten the egg, and smiled at her.

She smiled back. "Wow, that was fast."

"I had to learn to be fast. And the pizza will be here any minute."

"I could've answered the door, and paid for it."

"Yeah but I didn't want you to have to."

The doorbell rang, and she jumped.

"Be there in a minute," he called. He went and pulled on elastic waist shorts, and his holster for his side arm, then came back out, and headed for the door.

"Do you always do that?" she asked.

"Do what?"

"Answer the door armed."

"Sweetheart, I'm usually armed. And when I'm not, it's never far away."

"Oh," she said.

That could take some getting used to. But she had to admit; it did make her feel very safe.

He paid for the pizza, and then took it, and closed the door. He carried the pizza in, and put it on the coffee table in front of the couch.

"You get to pick the movie," he said. "Bring the waters, and come on."

His couch was very comfy, and after she ate two pieces of pizza, and had cuddled up next to him, she smiled, as she felt safe and happy with him.

He said, "I'm glad to see you're doing better."

"I'm just happy to be alive," she said. "Really happy."

"Seeing you happy makes me happy," he said, then kissed the top of her head.

Curled beneath the soft warm throw blanket he'd had on the back of the couch, she fell asleep before the movie was over.

When his cell phone went off, he reached for it, and saw it was his grandmother.

Answering it right away, before it could wake Zarifa, he said, "Hello grandma."

"Tony," she said. "I saw on the news about the shooting. I had to call you, to see if you're all right."

"I'm fine grandma. You'll never guess what I'm doing."

"Now don't give your grandma a heart attack here. Are you in the hospital?"

"No, I'm unscratched," he said. "But I have to be quiet, because, I'm holding an angel right now."

"This one is not one of those strippers."

"No, she's far from that. She's a high value woman, and I'm going to take very good care of her."

"Well, it's about time. When do I get to meet this angel?"

"I'll talk to her about that, and see when she can take some time off, for a little vacation."

"Is this the girl you talked to on the phone, when you came to visit?"

"Yes, grandma."

"I thought you might have found a good one. I'm glad."

"When I bring her to visit, I want you to promise me something."

"What is it?"

"I want you to promise, no more talking about grandbabies. I don't want you to scare her away with it."

"Does this one not like children?"

"She loves children. She teaches them gymnastics."

"Then she is healthy enough to have her own?"

"Grandma." His voice was warning her.

"I'll promise not to say a word near her about it, until after the wedding."

"Slow down, grandma. This is what I mean about scaring her away."

"What, she has something against marriage?"

"There needs to be an engagement first. I have to get her to say yes."

"I promise you, if you bring her here, I'll show her everything good about this family," she said. "Then she will want to marry you! She will not say no. You bring her, we will make it happen."

"Okay grandma. We have a deal."

"I'm glad you have not one scratch. And I'm glad you saved that girl. Is she your sleeping angel?"

"Yes, grandma, she is."

"I like her. She has a good heart. This Shimmy Mob, I do not understand it, but they are showing film clips from all around the world. It is a good thing, Tony boy. I like her already."

"Thanks grandma. She's going to love you too."

"I love you, Tony boy."

"I love you too, grandma."

"Bye bye," she said.

"Bye bye," he said, and hung up the phone.

He placed it back on the table, and looked down at his sleeping angel, her eyelashes resting against her skin, no makeup, and those bruises nearly faded away.

*She really is beautiful.*

He could hardly believe she was here, in his arms.

His grandmother was right, she had a good heart.

*Instead of staying in a victim mindset, which she could so easily have done, she'd stepped up to join Shimmy Mob, to help other women like herself, who'd been attacked.*

*She cares about others.*

He wouldn't mind spending the rest of his life protecting her, if she'd have him. He didn't want to lose her. And for one brief moment today, he might have.

SEALs didn't miss, but if the shooter had gotten one good shot off, before Cutter had known there was an imminent threat, it could've gone the other way.

Thank God it hadn't.

She might be an angel, but he wanted her here on earth, with him.

*Funny how near death could change you. Make everything crystal clear. Speed up time, and make you see your priorities.*

For the first time in his life, he was actively thinking about getting married. Meeting her had changed his life.

But he would take it slow.

*There's no rush. She deserves a slow courtship, and to be wooed, like the high value woman she is.*

He'd make sure they were suited for marriage together, and do the best thing, for both.

*It isn't easy being married to a SEAL.*

*A long engagement will be good. She'll need that, after that jerk off she'd been engaged to. She might need other things, to sort herself out. Maybe a counselor of some kind, to talk to.*

He would encourage that, and whatever else she might need.

*That Friday flower thing, Mrs. Brown talked about. That will be a good way to start this courtship. And I bet Mrs.*

*Brown will deliver them for me, when I'm deployed, so the pattern could be kept while I'm away.*

*Something steady that Zarifah could count on.*

It wasn't long after that thought, that he too drifted off to sleep. It had already been a very long day.

THE END

# Sample Chapter: Finding Bryce, Chapter One

Virginia Beach

"See you guys at Chicks?" Matthew Hunt "Matt" had opened the door, leaned in, and addressed Diesel and R.T. as they sat at two tables filling out paperwork.

"It's Kik's birthday," he reminded them.

Chicks Oyster Bar Marina was the favored place for SEAL Team Twelve to hang out when they were free to grab a beer and a bite to eat. Many celebrations through the years had been held there, from birthdays, to bachelor parties, and funeral wakes.

"Yeah," Tanner "Diesel" Taylor replied, then he held up the form he was filling out. "When these are done." He laid the paper down again and looked directly at Matt. "That was a clean op. Seems like there ought to be less paperwork instead of more, since we acquired the package and never had to fire one round."

Matt gave a nod, to acknowledge the comment and then said. "You're close to done. See you there."

A mostly by the book, no nonsense sort of man, dealing with what is, was his way. Matt wasn't likely to engage in any kind of discussion about how things ought to be.

Diesel didn't usually complain about things, but he wasn't in his usual mood today. He filled out one more line and then pushed the form across the table to his buddy, Reed "Railroad" Tindall. "We ought to be out running maneuvers, not stuck here in the office doing paperwork."

Reed hated that nickname and was stuck with it, but Diesel had his own nickname for his buddy, and called him R.T. 'Short for railroad tracks' is what he said if anyone asked.

Tanner didn't mind his nickname one bit. Tanner "Diesel" Taylor earned his nickname the first week of basic, when he showed up with grease stains under his fingernails.

Working at his dad's repair shop every week during high school, he'd despaired of his hands, and how the pretty girls would turn him down for dates, thinking his hands were dirty. They didn't know a mechanic could scrub and scrub his hands, and still have stains.

Although it didn't take long for his Navy and SEAL training to wash away those stains, the nickname stuck, along with his ability to repair just about any kind of engine, even in the dark.

In his mind, it was just another skill, but as he'd only followed in his father's footsteps for one year after high school, he was as proud of carrying on his father's legacy into the armed force, as he was of carrying the name.

All the men in his father's side of the family had been mechanics, and his grandfather, and great grandfather had served in the Army during World Wars I and II, which was where they'd learned the ability to work on engines in the dark.

It wasn't that he hadn't wanted to follow in their footsteps even down to their military service, it was that he'd wanted to do more.

Serving as a SEAL was more. Much more.

And he loved every minute of it.

After SEAL training, Diesel never had trouble getting dates again. He was now a lady magnet. Just one of the things his latest girlfriend had more than a little trouble with.

Last night, Kari had broken up with him again, which meant he was free to see whoever he wanted to see.

Diesel watched as R.T. pulled that damn letter out of his pocket again, and with a sad expression, prepared to read the letter again.

"Hey man, you're not going to read that letter again, are you?" Diesel could've repeated most of the letter, having heard it often enough.

"I just don't understand why Becky called it off. She never explained, and she won't answer my phone calls." R.T. bent his head to the letter.

*Damn. Dear John letters ought to be written in disappearing ink, or on exploding paper.*

Diesel kept his thoughts to himself, but shook his head. Watching R.T, he got an idea.

"Hey. Saturday night. Got plans?"

"Nope." R.T, kept reading." Got laundry."

"You've got plans now." Diesel said. "You can do laundry some other time."

R.T. raised his head, and looked at Diesel.

*Good. I got his attention away from that letter.*

"Picture lots of chicks in skimpy Halloween costumes," Diesel said.

R.T. groaned. "Costumes?"

"Yeah. Costumes. Don't worry. This will be fun. Costume party is a masquerade."

"I don't have a costume, and there's not enough time to put one together."

"Got you covered. I know a place that rents them, and they're open tonight."

"I don't know, man. I ought to try calling Becky again."

"Come on. This party is a much better time than doing laundry, and crying into your beer. Gonna be plenty of ladies at this party. You know how chicks dig costumes."

"Yeah." R.T. had to admit they did. "Thanks Diesel."

Diesel nodded. "Welcome."

R.T. put the letter away, before picking up the pen again, to finish his task.

It didn't take them long to finish. Then they went home to change clothes, with a plan to meet up at the bar.

After they'd arrived at Chicks, before the other guys arrived, they went to sit out on the deck, and startled a seagull who'd perched on the railing hoping to find food.

The seagull was often there, in that spot. So often, that tourists coming to the marina had started feeding it. Now it came every night, expecting to find food.

The waitress who appeared soon after, to take their orders, had named the bird Fred. She claimed "Fred just wants to be fed."

"What'll you have, guys?" Sheri asked, with a wide smile, between two dimples.

The little waitress was an adorable bundle of energy, and currently dating an airline pilot, who was gone not quite as often as a SEAL would be.

"When are you going to trade that boyfriend in, for a real SEAL?" Diesel teased, already knowing what her answer would be.

"You guys are gone too often, and too long," she said, with a shake of her head, and a laugh.

All the guys teased her this way, and Diesel knew she liked it, though her answer was always the same.

Diesel thought her answer was a lot of hooey. Commercial pilots were gone a lot too, and a woman who could handle that, could handle dating a SEAL.

Women who couldn't, likely wouldn't be able to handle their man being on the road, for any job.

*Some women needed more maintenance, just like some cars.*

Kari was one of those women. But he and Kari were through.

Diesel enjoyed watching the boats dock at the Marina, which took his mind off Kari just like knocking back a few beers with the guys would take R.T.'s mind off that damn letter.

Cutter, and Matt joined them, and took seats.

"I'll buy a round," "Cutter" Antonius (Tony) Cuttino said.

"What are we celebrating?" R.T. asked.

"My winning at the casino last weekend," Cutter said.

"You have Italian connections?" Sheri asked with a giggle.

The guys knew Cutter had cousins with connections to a casino in New Jersey. When he went home to visit his grandmother, he'd visit the casino and come back with his wins.

"Did you bring me back any cannoli?" Sheri asked.

Last time he'd brought back cannoli his grandma had made.

"Not this time," he said. "Next time, cannoli for you, sweet." He gave her a wink.

She blushed and smiled.

The men placed their beer orders, and she hurried to the bar for their drinks.

"Any of you guys going to the costume party Saturday?" Diesel asked.

"Yeah," Matt said. "I'm gonna go as an IRS auditor."

"Really, man?" R.T. said. "What kind of costume is that?"

"An easy one. Just wear a suit and tie, and carry a calculator," Matt shrugged. "I even got business cards made up to hand out." He reached into his pocket, pulled one out, and handed it to R.T. "I'm here to audit your tax records," he said.

R.T. took the card, and glanced down at it. "That would scare the hell out of a lot of people," he said.

"You are so weird," Diesel shook his head.

"It's simple, cheap, and easy, and I'll have fun with it," Matt said with a shrug.

"That's what costume parties are for," Diesel nodded. "Having fun."

Just after Sheri delivered the beers, Rich, Osprey, and Enrique "Kik" Garcia joined them on the deck, and more beers were ordered.

"Add on some onion rings," Diesel said.

Sheri nodded, and headed for the kitchen.

"You going to the costume party, Rich?" Diesel asked.

"Nah. Costume parties aren't my thing," Richard "Rich" Irvine said.

One of the oldest members of the group, he'd turned down most invites to socialize, since getting back in touch with an old girlfriend from high school at his high school reunion. Now he spent most of his free time with her, trying to get out of the friend zone. She was hesitant about dating a SEAL.

All but Rich would attend the costume party.

Osprey was going as Robin Hood, and would carry a primitive bow he hunted with for fun, and Kik was going as Superman.

"Superman?" R.T. said. "I would've thought you'd want to go as Zorro, or something like that."

"Why, because I'm Latino?" Kik shook his head. He smoothed his hair back with one hand, and then, reaching for a small section of his bangs, pulled it down, and made it curl. "I got the perfect hair. See? Superman."

All the guys laughed.

"Yeah, man," R.T. said. "I see it."

More SEAL brothers came in the door, which more than doubled the size of their gathering. The entire group was at Chicks tonight. All twenty SEALs.

Diesel glanced around the room. These twenty men were his brothers, and any one of them would have laid down his life for the other.

The Green Brotherhood was like no other, and he took a moment to take the sight of all his brothers in, creating a memory to savor in years to come.

The noise level in the bar rose, but the SEALs weren't the ones shouting and being rowdy.

They kept to themselves, and women in the bar were drawn to the strong silent warriors, like moths to flame. There was clearly something different about these men, the way they carried themselves, and the way they communicated amongst each other, often nonverbally, which set them apart. They exuded a quiet confidence, and their eyes were always taking in their surroundings with a quiet intelligence.

Craig McDonald "Big Mac" showed his Scots Irish heritage, by the multitude of freckles across his nose and cheeks, despite his deeply tanned face. It hid his ruddy complexion, and helped him blend in on their missions. Jet-black hair from his Irish mother saved him from having his fathers red hair, and allowed him to be picked for this special team.

To be on Team Twelve, you had to have dark hair as the team was often sent to South America, and needed to blend in. Blondes and redheads would stand out too much to be included. As a result, the men on Team Twelve could all be described as tall, dark, and handsome.

Blending in, in South America, was something Team Twelve did quite well.

Martin Lopez, the second Hispanic American on the team, was fluent in three languages, English, Spanish, and Portuguese. He was their go to man when it came to native dialects.

Chris Fenner "Fen" had almost gone to college on a chemistry scholarship, but he'd also wanted to become a SEAL. He was their best man with explosives, and a bit of a MacGyver, given his aptitude in chemistry.

He often said it was as much knowing what not to put together with another thing, as it was what to put together. He was also a pretty good cook, which he claimed also had to do with chemistry.

Daniel "Tractor" Edwards grew up on a hay farm, and would have been a fourth-generation farmer, if he'd stayed home on the farm instead of joining the SEALs.

His father had a John Deere collection that men traveled miles to see. Daniel had made the mistake of talking about it too often, early in his training, was handed the nickname "Tractor" and it stuck.

His best buddy in training told him it could've been worse; they could've saddled him with "Farm-boy."

Adam "DaVinci" Burgess was always drawing and doodling, with a pen, or pencil. Tonight, he was already drawing on his cocktail napkin before he'd finished his first beer.

It would have been easy to sit and watch him, instead of focusing on the hot young woman standing nearby, hoping for attention.

Thomas (Tom) Campbell "Soupman" got his nickname after explaining the way to spell his last name, was "Like the soup, man." Once the nickname stuck it was stuck good.

Scott Roberts, "Casper" was like a ghost. He could enter a room and then leave it, without anyone knowing he'd been there.

James Slater "Slim Jim" was a skinny man with toned muscles. His metabolism was so high, he could eat anything and not gain one pound of weight.

Sawyer "Pipes" Ferguson played the bagpipes with the local Scottish group, and sometimes wore a kilt, if performing with the group for weddings or funeral services.

Sam Valente, an Italian American known as "Sammie the Conductor" because of the expressive way he used his hands when he talked, was gesturing animatedly tonight, something he did when he'd drank enough beer.

Peter "Buzz" Horne had a weird snore that sounded like a low buzz.

Jocko "Numbers" Lewis was so good with numbers, they didn't need a calculator when he was around.

And Jake Summers "Oscar" could act any part, and make it believable.

But really, all these men were actors capable of blending in, making anyone believe they were who they pretended to be, and doing what it took to complete a mission.

They were a special team of Navy SEALs, one that few outside the SEAL Teams had ever heard of.

Tonight, they were all at the bar, because it was the rotation of their cycle to have them back in Virginia, before they cycled out again into the next phase. And it just happened to be Kik's birthday.

The beer was flowing, the noise level was rising, and if the good time Kik seemed to be having was any indication, he was going to have a huge hangover tomorrow.

Ordinarily, had he been back home with his family, there would have been a large family party, with a barbecued goat, music, and beer. After he joined the SEAL team, he'd continued to invite every one of his brothers to celebrate his birthday, and if they were available, they would join in.

Kik was having the time of his life tonight.

All the men trained hard, worked hard, and partied hard.

By the end of the evening, they made sure Kik made it home safe, as he was in no shape to drive, and the bar emptied out, the only occupant left on the patio, a lone seagull with the nickname of Fred, who had returned, hoping for leftovers to eat.

"Come on Pippa, this is the best party of the year, and everyone will be in costume," Cheryl said. "No one will know who you are. It's the perfect chance."

It was only the tenth time Cheryl had asked her to go to the Halloween party.

Finally, tired of being bugged about it, Pippa said, "Okay, I'll go."

"Great!" Cheryl's eyes widened, and she grabbed both of Pippa's hands, squeezing tight as she bounced on her heels. "You're going to be so glad you changed your mind. We're going to have a blast."

For once, Pippa would take a page from her mother's diary, and live in the moment.

As her mother had said, "Joyce, my dear, you haven't yet learned that life must be grasped in the moment."

Joyce Pippalousa Smith never gave out her birth name. Her full middle name had always been an embarrassment to her, though she did like her daddy's nickname for her.

He was the only one to call her "Pippa", and she missed him dearly. Her mother had always called her Joyce.

After her mother had made her announcement, she'd gone sailing off to Hawaii with a new man, who kept a boat at his summer home. "Waiting just gives you more likelihood you'll miss out. Your father may be dead, but I'm not."

Her mother was the kind of woman who couldn't stand to be alone, and one of her friends had been waiting in the wings, ready to date her.

Thinking back to the huge blow-up Pippa and her younger sister, Jeanie Magic Smith, had with their mother the day before their mother left town, made Pippa wonder where her mother was now, and reminded her, she needed to call Jeanie this weekend, and get caught up.

*Mother could be anywhere. I have no idea how to reach her at sea. I don't even have her new number.*

But as Jeanie often said, 'The phone works both ways.' And her sister's number hadn't changed.

Though usually Pippa was the one who had to call her sister. Months could go by, if she didn't, before Jeanie got around to calling her.

For once, Pippa was going to take a page from her mother's book. She was going to live a little.

It had been a long time since she'd gone out and had fun, and she'd always loved costume parties and Halloween.

"Now, what are you gonna be?" Cheryl asked.

"I don't know. I haven't had time to think about it," Pippa said, her tone wry. She'd only agreed a second ago.

Cheryl waved a hand, and continued in her rapid-fire way; clearly thrilled Pippa was going. "We can go to the costume shop after we get off work."

"Okay," Pippa said.

A masquerade party seemed safe enough. It was unlikely that her ex would be there. She'd moved several states away from Stan Nitty, and hoped to never see him again.

* * *

After work, they headed to That Magical Place, a store which sold costumes, and decorations for Halloween.

"Do you have any sexy costumes for women?" Cheryl asked.

The clerk grinned. "Yes, we do. Follow me, and I'll show you. Do you have any themes in mind?"

"I looked up your selections online. I think I'd like to be a woodland fairy," Pippa said. "With wings, and pointed ears, and everything." Now that she was getting excited about going, why not go full-on fantasy?

"Oh, fun," Cheryl said. "I'm going as a sexy nurse. Maybe I can play nurse with one of those hot Navy SEALs tomorrow night. Is your costume going to be sexy?"

"Well..." Pippa considered the costume she remembered from the website. "It's short and shows a lot of leg, and a lot of cleavage. It's also cheap, which I need. I don't have much budget for a costume."

"Want me to help you with your makeup and hair?"

"Oh, would you? That would be awesome." Pippa knew Cheryl was good at doing hair and makeup.

"Yeah, I'll come over an hour before and help you get ready," Cheryl said.

"Thanks, Cheryl." As she did every day, Pippa thanked her instincts for bringing her here to Virginia. Her sister had been only too willing to give her safe harbor when she'd needed it, and she lived just an hour away.

"No problem, Miss Pipp."

Pippa wrinkled her nose. "You're not gonna call me that at the party, I hope."

"No, I'm not gonna call you at all, 'til we agree it's time to go home. We're gonna circulate as single ladies, so the men will be more likely to approach us," Cheryl winked.

"Oh, right," Pippa nodded. "Good thinking."

* * *

The next day, Pippa's cousin Louise called her at work and left a message for her to call back. Far from being a normal call, Louise would only have called if someone had died or something very big had happened. So as Pippa called

Louise back, she held her breath. "Hey, Louise. What's happened?"

"This time it's good news, Pippa," Louise said. "You won't have to worry about Stan anymore. He's been sent to prison for three years. Felonious assault. He beat up a guy in a bar. That was bad enough. But then he went back and beat him some more. The guy was hurt bad, and they had to call an ambulance. Stan claimed it wasn't his fault, and the other guy did this and did that, but everything was caught on the bar's security cameras. And it didn't hurt that they had pictures of the bruises he left on your neck, or that you have a restraining order out on him, already on record. He's obviously a violent and dangerous man. I'm so glad he's been sent to prison and won't be out for a long time. I couldn't wait to tell you."

Pippa breathed a sigh of relief. Stress began to drain out of her body. "Oh, that is good news. He can't find me now, and suddenly show up on my doorstep to hurt me. Not while he's in prison. So, I'm safe. Finally. No more looking over my shoulder, worrying he might be the man in the baseball cap behind me. I'm safe, finally safe!"

She felt like dancing and spinning around the room.

"Yes, you are," Louise said. "Does this mean you'll come home, now?"

"I am home," Pippa said. "Virginia is my home now, and I just started taking a couple college classes."

"So, you're staying?"

"Yes." Pippa didn't say that she never wanted to move back to her hometown, but she surely felt that way. She'd escaped a horrible marriage, a depressing house, and a town, which lost more jobs every year, and she never wanted to go back.

There was no future there. Only the past. And the past was over and done. Finally.

"Well, all right. If that's what you want," Louise said. "I just want you to be happy."

"Oh, I am happy," Pippa said. "Happier than I've been in a very long time."

* * *

The night of the party, Pippa let Cheryl into her apartment, and they went straight into her bathroom, where she had a curling iron already plugged in. She wanted to look different tonight, and her long brown hair usually hung straight. Most days, she loved a wash-and-go kind of lifestyle and rarely wore makeup. But tonight, she wanted a little glamour—her hair curling, smoky-sparkling makeup, and fairy ears glued onto her ears.

Cheryl curled Pippa's hair until it had ringlets at the ends, which gave it a whole lot more body. Once she finished applying makeup to Pippa's face, Cheryl took gold glitter and sprinkled it in Pippa's hair and across her bared shoulders. Spaghetti straps held the silky fairy dress up, leaving a lot of skin bare. The way the dress was cut in back, there was no way to wear a bra with this one.

It was the most daring thing Pippa had ever worn in public.

"Might as well use it up," said Cheryl before sprinkling the rest of the vial of glitter down Pippa's cleavage.

Pippa felt the glitter whisper between her breasts. "Cheryl!" she said, laughing. "I don't need it everywhere."

"Oh, but I think you do," Cheryl said. "Keep him looking for the end of that glitter trail, and you'll have his attention for sure. Then he'll be hard at attention, and you'll have some real fun."

Pippa kept chuckling. "I'll bedazzle him with my cleavage."

"You know it." Cheryl winked and tossed the empty container into the trashcan. "Ready to go?"

"Yes, I just need my tiny purse."

"Here." Cheryl reached into her purse for two condoms and handed them to Pippa. "Be prepared, because those Navy boys are not always like boy scouts, and some of them really get around."

"Oh, right." They hadn't talked much about Pippa's former life, only that she'd divorced a man who was no good and that she was trying to make a new life without complications. She hadn't hinted at her ex's violent tendencies.

Cheryl, being a party girl, understood the "no complications" bit. She never dated a guy longer than six months. Said it got claustrophobic if they lingered any longer.

"Thanks. I hadn't thought to pick those up," Pippa said.

"Always keep one in your purse and some in your nightstand. Tonight's a chance for you to have fun without the hassle of a date. But if you need more than two of these, you're on your own, girlfriend."

Unable to stop a blush, Pippa shook her head. "I won't need more than two."

*I'll be lucky to need one*, she thought. It had been over a year since she'd had sex, and she missed it. In the good times, at the beginning of her marriage, before everything went terribly bad, sex had been good, with that rush of attraction that went straight to her core, lighting everything up, just like fairy lights. It had been magic.

*I want that again, even if for just one night. This is a start. And no one will even know who I am. This is perfect.*

# Sample Chapter: Real Movie Hero Chapter One

Reed "Railroad" Tindal aka "R.T." sat outside on the deck of Chicks bar, at the marina, enjoying his beer, as he and two of his SEAL brothers watched a boat pulling into one of the slips.

It was a perfect evening for sailing. Just enough of a breeze and the sun starting to set.

"That's the life," "Cutter" Antonious (Tony) said. "What I'm going to do after I retire. Nothing but sails, suds, and sweethearts."

"A girl for you in every port," Tanner "Diesel" Taylor said. "Not much different from what you have now."

Diesel liked to have a beer in every port, but Cutter, he was all about the women.

Around SEALs there were always women. Drawn to them like moths to flames.

A seagull landed on one of the posts near them and looked at them for food.

Sheri, their favorite cheerful dimpled waitress, showed up again to see if the men wanted another beer. "Fred has joined your party," she said. "Do you want some pretzels for him? And another beer?"

Reed shook his head. "Sorry, guys, I'd hang for another beer and to stay and chat," Reed said, "but I'm headed out to see a movie premiere."

"Oh, lucky you," Sheri said.

"Which one?" Diesel asked.

"*Turn and Deliver*, with Cole Kennick," Reed said.

"He's very handsome," Sheri said. "I like his movies."

"There should be plenty of good action scenes in that one," Cutter said. He raised his nearly empty glass. "And I'll take another beer, hun."

She smiled her dimpled grin at him. "You've got it."

"Cole Kennick does a better job keeping it real than most," Reed said.

"How'd you get passes?" Diesel asked.

"Won them from the local radio station," Reed said. "I've got one unclaimed pass." He turned to their waitress. "If you'd like to go, Sheri."

"You know I can't," Sheri shook her head. "My boyfriend wouldn't like that."

"It's just a movie," Reed said. "Not a kiss."

She put one hand on her hip. "Now you know that movies lead to kisses, and that is how people get into trouble."

"Are you saying you couldn't keep yourself from kissing me?" Reed teased.

Throwing one hand in the air she said, "Now you know that's not what I meant." Shaking her head, she turned and walked away.

"Well, guys, looks like I have one pass up for grabs if one of you wants it," Reed said.

"Can't tonight," Cutter said. "I'm meeting a chick here."

"That does not surprise me," Reed said.

"Another hot dancer with long legs?" Diesel asked.

Cutter grinned. "You know it."

The man was predictable as hell when it came to women, and he always seemed to be dating a dancer.

Reed turned to Diesel. "Do you want it?"

"Dad is flying in tonight, and I'm picking him up at the airport," Tanner "Diesel" Taylor said. "So, this is my limit tonight." He raised his beer. "And I've got to go." He drained his beer, and then pushed his chair back to stand.

Reed stood and said good night to both before heading toward the door.

*Too bad the extra ticket would go to waste.*

He'd just picked the tickets up from the station before heading to Chicks so there hadn't been time to ask around. Plus, he hadn't figured on both his brothers being busy tonight.

It was a weeknight, not a Saturday, and generally they all hung out at Chicks enjoying the views and brews. Tonight, it had just been the three of them.

It looked like he was headed to the premiere alone. But that didn't bother him. He would enjoy the movie either way.

* * *

"I can't go tonight," Tanya told Christie over the phone, her voice hard to hear, while Tanya's dog, Brutus, whined in the background, and her cat, Miss Priss, meowed mournfully. "There's no way I'll make the movie premiere. I hate to let you down, but it's crazy here."

"Oh, no," Christie said, her stomach dropping to her toes. "What's going on?"

*Tanya is bailing.*

Dismayed, Christie glanced at her watch. *We're supposed to meet in front of the theater in twenty minutes.*

The movie premiere passes Christie had won last week from the local radio station were only good for tonight's premiere.

*It's too late to call someone else.*

Christie looked down at her red and white dress which showed off her curves.

*And I'm dressed forties style. There's no time to change clothes.*

The whole idea was she and Tanya were going to have a "girls' night out," dressed in 1940's attire. First, they'd see the movie, and then they'd go for drinks afterward. Both women enjoyed dressing in vintage fashions, and they'd each bought new dresses to show off.

Christie couldn't help but be disappointed.

Tanya interrupted Christie's thoughts. "Cole Kennick has to be the hottest man in Hollywood, and you know how much I wanted to go to the premiere with you. But Miss Priss just yakked all over my bedspread, right after I finished cleaning up after Brutus. They're both sick. I'm thinking I might need to call the vet."

"I'm so sorry. Are they going to be all right?" Christie's concern for the animals pushed aside her disappointment at her best friend bailing on her. "Do you want me to come over?"

"No, I can handle this," Tanya said. "You go on to the movie. I don't want to be the reason you miss the premiere."

"What do you think it is?" Christie asked. "Did they both get into something? Maybe eat something bad?"

"They've eaten something I didn't give them, that much I do know," Tanya said. "What it is though, I can't tell."

"Oh my god." Christie didn't say her next thought.

*Poison. The nasty neighbor might've poisoned them.*

Tanya's neighbor was always complaining about Brutus and his barking. Brutus was a German Shepard and very protective of Tanya. Tanya's crazy neighbor jumped at any excuse to call the police. On the other hand, Miss Priss was a beautiful white Persian cat who never bothered anyone, although she did shed white hair everywhere.

"You'd better take a sample of the puke to the vet, in case he needs to test what they got into," Christie said.

"Already thought of that. Go enjoy the movie," Tanya said, her tone reassuring. "Don't worry. I don't want to ruin your fun evening."

"You're not going to ruin my evening," Christie said. "But I will miss you."

"Well, you'd better hurry or you'll be late," Tanya said. "And I don't think they let you in late to premieres."

Christie sighed. "All right, but I'm calling you just as soon as the movie is over."

"Thanks, Christie. And again, I'm so sorry about this."

"It's okay," Christie said. "You just take care of those sweet fur babies."

"Thanks for understanding," Tanya said.

"Hey, that's what best friends do," Christie said.

"Thanks bestie," Tanya said. "Chat soon. Don't be late!"

"I won't, "Christie said. "Bye."

"Bye."

Worrying about Tanya's fur babies, Christie grabbed the movie passes and hurried out the door to her car.

Fortunately, she made every streetlight by driving two miles under the speed limit and arrived just in time.

The line inside the Cinema One complex was long and filled the lobby. Christie stood at the end of line waiting.

*At least I only need one seat.*

Two ticket takers stood at the entrance. A man and a woman. The woman held a basket to collect their cell phones. She was explaining that everyone would get their phones back when they came out of the movie and she'd always be with the phones. Taking the phones was to prevent anyone from sneaking to take a video of the movie. The woman reminded everyone that pirating was against federal law.

Christie handed the man her pass and placed her phone into the basket the woman held. As she moved away, her gaze lingered on her phone reluctantly.

*I hope Tanya won't need to reach me soon and that the vet tells Tanya her fur babies will be okay. She's got to do something about that mean neighbor. That woman has gone too far if she has poisoned them, and I'll bet she has. Poor Miss Priss and Brutus.*

Inside, the theater was semi-dark and nearly full.

Christie stood at the bottom of the theater's stadium seating, letting her eyes adjust to the darkness and looking for one good seat.

*Oh, there's one next to that fit, handsome man with the brown hair wearing the brown leather jacket.*

Her gaze stopped and held as he captured her attention. His build was solid. Strong. Something about him drew her attention—and then she noticed, he was looking right back at her with his intense hazel eyes. But then, his gaze swept past her to the other side of the theater, as he sat quietly scanning the room.

*Is he waiting for someone? Saving that seat? I hope not. It's a good location, and I'm running out of options.*

She headed for the seat, hoping it would be free.

Reaching his isle, she leaned forward, drawing his full attention, and asked, "Is this seat taken?"

"No." He shook his head, his eyes watching her.

She smiled, and the teenager seated on the end of the aisle moved his feet, so she could slip between the rows.

"Excuse me," she said, and began the "theater row shuffle", being careful, as she was wearing her highest heels. The new red ones, with the little bows on the front, and tall, narrow heels.

She'd had so much fun planning to glam it up on their girls' night out, and both she and Tanya had pretty dresses any pin-up girl would be proud of. Now, Tanya wouldn't see her in her new red and white checkered dress. The cool summer dress was form-fitting, and showed her curves, making her feel attractive, and glamorous, in a Marilyn Monroe kind of way.

*All dolled up for a night on the town, and no one to spend it with.*

There was no one here, that she knew, to see the dress and to appreciate it along with the time and effort she'd spent on her blonde hairdo, and makeup to complete the look. Plenty of men had ogled her since she'd stepped out of her car, in the theater parking lot, but that wasn't the kind of attention she wanted.

Tanya would've appreciated the dress, and the time it took to find the perfect dress, and to do her hair and makeup just so. Still, the entire row of men she passed, and men in the rows behind them, watched her every move.

Stepping daintily to the left of the handsome man in the brown leather jacket, and in front of the empty seat, she turned and sat while trying to play it cool, like she just needed a seat and not like she'd hoped to sit with him. Wondering where to put her purse and keeping in mind how a movie theater floor could be sticky, she bent and placed her new, shiny red purse on top of her feet, balancing it on her toes.

The air-conditioning sent a cool draft across her bare shoulders, bringing goose bumps, and making her want to shiver. She'd forgotten how cool the air could be in a theater when she'd ordered this dress. Wishing she'd worn a shawl; Christie hoped all the people in the theater would create enough body heat to warm the room up. At least when she leaned back against the seat, the vent blew in front of her, not on her back. Though her neck and collarbone were receiving the draft, chilling her front side.

Now that she was seated, she realized how much taller than her the handsome man was. Sitting next to him made her feel downright delicate. His chest, shoulders, and arms were muscular, and he exuded strength.

*Oh my, but he's handsome, and he smells good.*

She glanced down at his hand.

*No wedding ring. I wonder why he's here without a date, or a friend? Women probably fall all over him. I wonder what his name is.*

On her other side, a large man in an orange T-shirt and jeans sat holding a huge tub of popcorn. "Here by yourself?" he said. "That's terrible."

Taken aback by his sly tone, she leaned away from the nosy man and closer to the handsome man, aware of him now watching her and the nosy man.

"Why would you ask?" she said, frowning and then catching herself, as she decided she shouldn't be speaking to this stranger about whether she was out alone. "That's none of your business," she said, feeling herself bristle.

*Maybe this seat wasn't such a good one after all.*

Though the view of the screen was excellent, and she

was near enough to the aisle to get out without having to climb over half a row of people, now she hoped the nosy man wouldn't continue to bother her.

Mr. Nosy leaned forward, as if to say something else, and his hand reached toward her, but then he stopped, looking past her to handsome man.

She turned to glance at handsome man, wondering what he'd done to stop Mr. Nosy.

Handsome Man's hair was damp, likely from having taken a recent shower. Hot as it was outside, his hair would've dried otherwise. She became aware once again of his aftershave or cologne, a manly enticing scent.

"Most people are here because they received a pass to the premiere," the handsome man said dryly.

Mr. Nosy shut up and went back to eating his popcorn, taking a huge handful.

Christie exhaled stress she didn't know she'd been holding.

*Better Mr. Nosy keeps his attention on his popcorn, and not on me.*

"Thank you," Christie whispered under her breath, just low enough the handsome man could hear.

"No problem," came his low answer.

*He smells good.*

And that low voice was doing things to her insides as his scent assaulted her senses on another level. Pheromones flooded her body, making her aware of her breath, her heartbeat, the way her palms were starting to warm. The slight flush in her pale cheeks dend chest, which always happened, would begin now.

Her pheromones could get her into trouble sometimes when they kicked in before she figured out if a guy was a good man to be with or not.

As the lights began to dim, she thought, *Good thing we'll be in a dark theater. Handsome Man will never know how I'm reacting to him.*

* * *

Reed Tindal sat scanning the crowd.

Attentiveness was by now an ingrained habit, though he was casual about it, unless he needed not to be.

A trained SEAL, when he was awake, he was always aware of his surroundings.

The pretty blonde with the creamy skin and stunning green eyes had caught his attention before she'd noticed him. Then their gazes had connected, and he'd felt that flicker, the one that always happened when attraction kicked in. This attraction was strong. Strong enough to take him by surprise, as she usually wouldn't have been his type.

She was wearing a delicate red and white checked dress with little straps and high heels.

With soft blonde shoulder length curls tied with a red ribbon, smokey eyeliner, and cherry red lipstick, she was girly from her head to her red painted toenails, which peeked out of her shoes. Those red high heeled shoes with red bows on the front were the kind that always made him wonder how a woman would run if she had to, without turning an ankle. He hoped this beauty never found out. She turned heads dressed like that, and some heads were best avoided.

He wondered what her story was, and why she was all dressed up to watch a movie by herself. There was a story there. He couldn't imagine any hot-blooded male standing up a woman who looked as good as she did.

Reed was used to dating women who were more practical. Sensible about things like shoes, wore jeans instead of dresses, and carried guns. There was nowhere on that pretty dress where this woman could carry a gun or anything else. In fact, he'd bet she didn't even know how to shoot a gun.

She looked like the "take care of me" type, not the "I'll take care of things myself" type.

Everyone was seated. A man in a black suit stepped onto the stage and welcomed them to the premiere, then the lights were dimmed, and everyone settled in to watch the show.

The blonde, caught up in the story, would catch her breath, only to release it when Cole escaped the bad guy's malevolence, and avoided getting so much as a mark on him.

Her breathy sighs and little gasps caught Reed's attention each time, though he was also focusing on the movie. He was good at doing two things at once.

The movie held her complete attention, and she seemed unaware of anything else, though Reed had noted her initial reaction to him.

Reed could have been caught up in the movie as well if he'd let himself. Cole was one of the few actors who did their own stunts, and he kept his movies more real than most. Which meant Reed didn't disengage and start critiquing action shots five minutes into the movie.

Had he been at home, he might have been as caught up as the woman was. But out in public, nothing would ever take up his total attention. However, that was not to say he wasn't enjoying the movie. In fact, he was enjoying the movie as well as her reactions to it.

*Total opposites*, he thought as he noted her reactions to the movie. She was so caught up in the movie, she didn't notice anything else.

Reed had grown up in a neighborhood where boys had

to fight, or be picked on, so he'd learned early on to fight, and to pay attention to who was where, always. He viewed her as he would a child, or any other innocent civilian, who hadn't learned to be wary. He was glad to see her relaxing and enjoying the movie.

This was why men like him fought. To protect the innocent, and preserve a peaceful way of life, and freedom. These were some of the reasons he fought.

Actor Cole Kennick played roles in which he did the same, which was one reason Reed enjoyed watching his movies.

Some feeling he couldn't have named, other than to call it a sixth sense, made him turn his focus to a man at the front of the theater, dressed all in black.

*Not one of the staff.*

Another patron, perhaps.

He stood at the far-right corner of the theater. Something about him was very off.

The man turned to face the crowd, and began to move his arm upward —

*Damn.*

Reed went calm and cool, even as he thought the word, his training kicking in, knowing the man was going to shoot.

Everything around Reed slowed.

"Everyone down!" he yelled, as his hand landed on the pretty blonde's shoulder, forcing her to the ground behind the seats.

The shooter raised his gun to fire.

# Afterword

Thank you for taking the time to read *Saving the Bellydancer*. If you enjoyed my story, please consider telling your friends and or posting a review.

Word of mouth is an author's best friend and much appreciated. Reviews are so important for authors. If you would be so kind as to leave a review and a rating on any website, this is the best way to give back and encourage authors whose work you have enjoyed.

Please know that I appreciate and read every single review.

Infinite love and gratitude.

Debra Parmley

# What is Shimmy Mob?

The inaugural Shimmy Mob was held on May 1st, 2011. Shimmy Mob members support domestic abuse shelters worldwide, with an annual bellydance flash mob, to raise awareness of domestic abuse and shelter locations. Sabeya, the founder of Shimmy Mob, intended to hold the event one time only, as a fund raiser for local women's shelters. The response to the event was unanimous: do it again.

Each year, on International Bellydance Day, all around the world, Shimmy Mob members dance, wearing matching shirts, dancing our choreography for the year to the selected song as a fund raising event. To learn more, visit: https://shimmymob.com/

# Acknowledgments

Thank you to all who helped make this book happen, and who have helped me share this story, and Shimmy Mob, with the world.

Thank you, Francesca Sabeya Anastasi, for creating Shimmy Mob and for being such an inspirational leader.

To all my Memphis Shimmy Mob assistants, and all the Team Leaders, who came after me, to help our local domestic abuse shelter and to help the women and children who came through the shelter.

And to all my dance sisters throughout the world, from those who joined Shimmy Mob from the first year in 2011 and each year after.

You know the meaning of sisterhood and you know how to love your neighbor.

Though I no longer live in one location, as we move across the U.S. in our motorhome, my heart dances with you, even when my feet can't dance beside you.

Sabeya, you made me want to share a Shimmy Mob story with the world, and so I did, and we know what this one small ripple in the waters has already done, when the book was previously titled *Protecting Zarifah*. Thank you for sharing that story in the interview.

To all my Shimmy Mob Sisters, and those I met in my Shimmy Mob and Bellydance journeys.

To all who've supported the cause and my books.

Now as to the writing of the book and the production side, my thanks ...

To Bobby, who helped with the gun scene.

To my editors and early readers who wanted more of this story. You will have known it as, *Protecting Zarifah*, when it was part of Susan Stokers Operation Alpha series. When the rights were returned to me, in August 2022, I then revised the book to fit into a new setting as part of my new SEAL series world, The Green Brotherhood: SEA Team XII. There, the book will now stay.

To Sheri L. McGathy, my cover artist.

To retired Navy SEAL Bill Hellman, who advised me on the creation of my new SEAL Team series, The Green Brotherhood: SEAL Team XII as I incorporated this revised story into the series.

Thank you to my family, and especially my husband, for love and support through all these journeys and adventures we've been through.

Special thanks to all my readers. I've loved being able to share this story with you, to give you a glimpse into the world of Shimmy Mob Bellydance. To those who are new to Shimmy Mob, you will find a page with a link to learn more.

My infinite love and gratitude to you all.

- Debra Parmley

# About the Author

Author Debra Parmley believes "Every day we are alive is a beautiful day," and she likes to give her readers and her story people a story that ends happily.

An Air Force veteran's wife, Debra writes military romantic suspense, contemporary romance, historical romance, poetry, and memoir.

Debra married her high sweetheart, whom she asked out after a five-dollar bet. After living in five states with her husband and their two sons, and then living 23 years just outside Memphis, TN, she and her husband sold everything and now live and travel the U.S. in their 43-foot motorhome.

Debra is an adventurous writer who has sold travel and has walked the plank of a pirate ship off the coast of Grand Cayman. She has gone swimming with dolphins in Moorea in French Polynesia, has escorted a bus full of people through Scotland, and has set foot in 13 countries. She even climbs lighthouses because she is afraid of heights.

You can see read about her travels on her Beautiful Day Traveler blog. https://beautifuldaytraveler.wordpress.com/

As Debra Bishop, she writes fairy tales for all ages, fantasy, and children's books.

Visit www.debraparmley.com

# Also by Debra Parmley

**Military Romantic Suspense:**

**Green Brotherhood SEAL Team XII:**

Finding Bryce, book one - eBook, paperback

Real Movie Hero, book two - eBook, paperback

Saving the Bellydancer, book three - eBook, paperback

**Brotherhood Protectors series:**

Montana Marine - eBook, paperback

Defensive Instructor - eBook, paperback

Marine Protector - eBook, paperback

Blind Trust - eBook, paperback

A Triple C Ranch Christmas Wedding - eBook, paperback

Montana Delta Rescue - eBook, paperback

Montana SEAL Protector - eBook, paperback

Montana White Horse Wedding - eBook, paperback - 2023

Montana Rodeo Protector - eBook, paperback – 2023

**Bobbins Sisters Trilogy:**

Check Out – book one, eBook, paperback, audiobook

Check In – book two, eBook, paperback

Check Up – book three, 2023

**Single Title:**

Aboard the Wishing Star - eBook, paperback, audiobook

Jenna's Christmas Wish - eBook, paperback

To Catch an Elf – 2023

## Western Historical Romance:

Gone to Texas: A Desperate Journey - (original sweeter version) - Large Print Hardcover, eBook, paperback

Dangerous Ties - eBook, paperback, audiobook

Deadly Adversaries - eBook, paperback

Desperate, Dangerous, Deadly: A Western Collection – eBook

Isabella, Bride of Ohio: American Mail Order Bride – (original sweeter version) - Large Print Hardcover, eBook, paperback

## 1920's Romance:

**Butterflies Fly Free series:**

Trapping the Butterfly – book one, eBook, paperback, audiobook, Large Print Hardcover

Dancing Butterfly – book two, eBook, paperback

Exotic Butterfly – book three, 2023

## Fairy Tale Romance:

The Twelve Stitches of Christmas – (short story) – eBook

## Futuristic/Dystopian Romance:

**The Hunger Roads Trilogy:**

Another Change of Scenery – 2023

Down a Back Road – 2023

Into the Convergence Zone – 2024

**Poetry Anthology:**

Twilight Dips – eBook, print

**Nonfiction Memoir:**

Anywhere But Here: Our First Year Living on the Road - 2023

**Out of Print:**

Protecting Pippa

Split Screen Scream

Protecting Zarifah

Vague Directions – short story

A Desperate Journey

Isabella, Bride of Ohio

Tales of Deadwood - anthology

We Know the Truth, Do You? Area 51 – anthology (going to the moon/time capsule)

Wounded Heroes - anthology

Hansel & Gretel: Down the Rabbit Hole – anthology

More Monsters from Memphis – anthology

**Also writing as Debra Bishop:**

**Fairytales for all ages:**

The Sweetest Day - fairytale Hansel and Gretel story, eBook,
paperback

## Fantasy:

The Rolling House – time travel serial fiction on Kindle Vella

Gatalop – 2023

Bellserie – 2023

Children's stories coming in 2023

www.ingramcontent.com/pod-product-compliance
Lightning Source LLC
Chambersburg PA
CBHW030755200726

48288CB00004B/1189